W9-BYG-185

Baltimore Chronicles

Volume 4

Baltimore Chronicles

Volume 4

Treasure Hernandez

www.urbanbooks.net

Urban Books, LLC
78 East Industry Court
Deer Park, NY 11729

Baltimore Chronicles Volume 4 Copyright © 2012
Urban Books, LLC

All rights reserved. No part of this book may be reproduced in any form or by any means without prior consent of the Publisher, excepting brief quotes used in reviews.

ISBN- 13: 978-1-60162-482-6
ISBN- 10: 1-60162-482-4

First Trade Paperback Printing March 2012
Printed in the United States of America

10 9 8 7 6 5 4 3 2 1

This is a work of fiction. Any references or similarities to actual events, real people, living, or dead, or to real locales are intended to give the novel a sense of reality. Any similarity in other names, characters, places, and incidents is entirely coincidental.

Distributed by Kensington Publishing Corp.
Submit Wholesale Orders to:
Kensington Publishing Corp.
C/O Penguin Group (USA) Inc.
Attention: Order Processing
405 Murray Hill Parkway
East Rutherford, NJ 07073-2316
Phone: 1-800-526-0275
Fax: 1-800-227-9604

Chapter 1

Neighbors, who needs them?

Scar's eyes popped open. "These mu'fuckin' birds!" He had been woken up for the fifth day in a row by a flock of birds chirping outside his bedroom window.

"I hate the fuckin' country," he mumbled to himself as he wiped his eyes and lumbered out of bed. The bright morning sun was shining through the south-facing window of his bedroom. He stood and looked out that same window at the black birds cawing in the tree. "I'm putting an end to this bullshit once and for all." Still groggy from his sleep, he put on a pair of cream-colored sweat pants with a matching zip-up hoodie.

He had only been in the country house for a week, but to him it felt like a year. He hated the slow pace and solitude. There was no action, no one around, and no fun. In short, he was bored out of his mind.

The first few days at the house were not so bad. He had been occupied by all the action of moving in. Being the head of the biggest drug cartel in Baltimore had its advantages. He had some of his low-level soldiers come out to move his shit, while his top-level soldiers sat down for a meeting about how things would run. Scar told them that Flex would be representing him in the city while he was hiding out in the country.

Although Flex hadn't been with Scar's crew for very long, he showed loyalty and drive, the two things that Scar demanded. Scar noticed and rewarded Flex with a promotion. Scar felt that Flex had grown into a man—especially the way he handled killing Sticks after Scar found out that Sticks had stolen money from him. Scar had seen a definite change in Flex's demeanor after the young soldier got a taste of murder, so now, whatever Flex said was word. If any of them had a problem with Flex, then they would have a problem with Scar.

If Day had been at the house, he would have been representing Scar, but that nigga had disappeared. At one time, Day was Scar's right hand man, but what Scar didn't know was that Day had ulterior motives. Day had infiltrated his posse and become his right hand man, all the while scheming to take down Scar's empire. Now Day was nowhere to be found. Since Scar had been in the country, he hadn't seen or heard from him. As a matter of fact, no one in his crew had. Finding out what happened to Day was one of the things on Scar's list. He just hadn't been able to investigate since his sudden escape from Baltimore.

Fully awake now, Scar went to his closet and pulled out his AK-47. He inserted a magazine full of bullets and cocked the side handle. The machine gun was loaded and waiting to inflict some serious damage. This was the last thing Scar wanted to be doing. He wanted to still be sleeping, but he'd had enough. Every morning some damn birds were interrupting his sleep, and he was sick of it.

The rest of the house was quiet as he walked out the front door into the early morning chill. He carefully and quietly walked around the house so he didn't alert the birds to his presence. They could be as loud as they wanted, and Scar hoped they would be. He figured if they remained loud, it would drown out any noise he made and it would be easier to ambush them.

"Enjoy your last chirps, you mu'fuckin' squawking crows." He raised the machine gun, propped the butt end against his shoulder, and aimed at the middle branches of the tree. A shower of bullets spit out of the gun barrel as Scar pulled the trigger. Bullet shells flew every which way and littered the ground. He sprayed the tree back and forth as the air filled with the smell of spent gunpowder. The black birds scattered in an attempt to flee as they were bombarded with bullets. Some made it out and were able to fly away. Most got caught in the line of fire.

Forced to stop shooting because the magazine was spent, Scar dropped the gun to his side. He surveyed the damage he had inflicted. There were feathers and leaves still lingering in the air, taking their sweet time floating to the ground. They would settle next to the dead birds. Smoke from the gun barrel was swirling in and around the tree branches. There were at least twenty dead birds scattered around, lying in the grass.

Scar was proud as he stood admiring his work. "Now maybe I can get some sleep." He stood on top of the hill and looked over the valley that sprawled out in front of him. There were only treetops and sky as far as he could see. It was the most isolated he had felt since escaping the heat in Baltimore to hide out in the country.

This loneliness made him long for the good old days, when he was young and he and his brother Derek were inseparable. They looked out for one another. Even though they didn't have any parents and were in an orphanage, they had each other. They were family. Scar longed for that bond again. He had it for a while, until he started fucking Derek's wife, Tiphani. That act of betrayal had pushed Derek over the edge and destroyed any familial bond they once had. Now they were sworn enemies, and Scar had no one close to him. He didn't trust anyone. He had kept everyone at arm's length while becoming the biggest player in the game. Now that he was isolated and alone, he regretted sleeping with Tiphani and betraying his brother.

He stayed there for a good hour, thinking about his past. He went over everything that had happened and all of his actions that brought him to this place. He thought back to the elation and love he felt the first time he saw his brother again after years of separation. He thought about the first time he and Tiphani hooked up, and the time his brother Derek found him in bed with Tiphani. It was bad enough that he was fucking his brother's wife, but it was worse that he was doing it in his brother's bed. That discovery sparked the feud that turned Scar's world upside down.

Before that, Derek and Scar had worked together. Scar was on the side of crime, and Derek was on the side of the law, but they worked in tandem to make extreme amounts of money and control most of the drug trade in Baltimore. With his brother working against him now, wanting revenge, Scar was forced into hiding. The entire police force was on a manhunt for Scar. All of the politicians and police officers the he had been paying off stopped taking his bribes. He was poison in the city. Without any allies in high places, he had been forced to escape from Baltimore, eventually ending up here in the middle of nowhere.

"Fuck that. What's done is done. Can't change nothin' now." He snapped back to the present and walked into the house. He wasn't about to let sentimentality get the better of him. There was a reason he was the head of the most notorious gang in Baltimore.

Scar walked in the house to find his niece sitting at the kitchen table coloring in her coloring book. His nephew was on the floor in the living room playing with his toy cars. The kids were too young to realize that they were being held as captives. Scar had originally kidnapped the children to get his brother to help him escape Baltimore. Since Derek was a former detective, Scar figured he could find out when and where the police were searching for him.

He did escape Baltimore, but it was in no way because of any help Derek provided. If Scar hadn't taken initiative and left when he did, he would have been captured. As he was driving out of Baltimore, the authorities were driving to raid his house. This pissed Scar off to no end. He was now holding the kids as punishment for Derek and to try to shake Tiphani out of hiding. Scar wanted revenge on that bitch. He was going to make her pay for betraying him and trying to set him up at the armored car ambush.

"Hi, Uncle Scar," they said in unison as he walked through the door.

"What's up, little ones? Why you up so early?" He hid the gun behind his back as best he could.

"We heard some loud bangs outside," his nephew said. He was the younger of the two children.

"It sounded like firecrackers," said Scar's niece.

"That's what it was. Firecrackers. I was tryin'a scare away the loud birds outside my window," Scar replied. "Go upstairs and change out your PJs and I'll make y'all some breakfast."

"Pancakes!" yelled his nephew.

"Pancakes." Scar smiled his crooked smile. Even though he had kidnapped the kids, they were the only things that made Scar smile these days.

The kids raced up the stairs to see who could change the fastest. Scar followed them and put his machine gun back in the closet. Since they'd been with him, he had tried to hide the guns and drugs from them. He didn't want them growing up like he did. He wanted them to keep their innocence as long as they could.

Scar started mixing together the pancake batter and warming the griddle as the kids came rumbling down the stairs. "First!" His niece crashed into the table.

"Not fair. You always win." Scar's nephew pouted.

"You'll win one day, big man. How 'bout you get the first pancake?" Scar tried to cheer him up.

Scar served breakfast as the kids occupied themselves with their own little games. They had formed a tight bond since all of the drama surrounding their family started. First, their father, Derek, had been put in jail; then their mother, Tiphani, staged her own kidnapping and disappeared. Now their uncle had kidnapped them. They had been shielded from it as much as possible, but children are like dogs; they can sense when things aren't right. Kids are smarter than adults give them credit for.

"When is Mama and Daddy coming to get us?" the nephew asked.

Scar hesitated before he answered. "Soon, little man, soon."

"Maybe we should go back to Baltimore. They might not know where we are, or they might get lost," his niece chimed in.

"I wish we could go back to Baltimore, but this is home now. I talked to your pops the other day, and he still busy. He'll get here as quick as he can," Scar lied.

"I don't like it here. I want to go back home," said his nephew.

"Me too. Me too." Scar agreed.

A somber silence fell over the table, all of them sitting with their own thoughts. The kids were thinking about their parents and wishing they were in their own house. Scar was wishing he was back on familiar ground, bangin' on the streets of Baltimore.

Scar was getting the uneasy feeling that he may be stuck in the country for a long time. If that was the case, he needed to figure out what the hell he was going to do with the kids. He didn't want to become their father. When he kidnapped them, he hadn't thought about keeping them long term. He was thinking about the present and what he needed to do at that moment. The fuck did he know about raising kids? He couldn't look to his childhood as an example. He watched his mother get beaten to death and was in and out of foster homes his whole childhood—not to mention the fact that the state separated him and his brother while they were in foster care. He already felt like he was a father figure to some of these wild-ass soldiers in his crew. He didn't need two real children to take care of and send off to school.

Usually if Scar had a problem like this, he would just kill whoever it was that was clinging to him. He was hoping to come to another solution before he had to do that to the kids.

The doorbell rang and snapped everyone out of their thoughts.

"I'll get it," said the niece.

"No. You stay here," Scar instructed with a little force behind his words.

The kids obeyed, and Scar quietly and cautiously walked to the front window. He peeked out the window so as not to attract attention from whoever was at the door.

"Who the fuck?" Scar mumbled to himself.

He quietly walked back to the kitchen and told the kids to go play out back. They obeyed and went out the back door. Scar went into a cabinet and took out a 9 mm from the top shelf. He slipped it in his waistband as he walked back to the front door. As he approached, the stranger knocked on the door.

"Who is it?" Scar stood a little back and to the side of the door in case the person started shooting or tried to kick in the door.

"Oh, hello. It's your neighbor," the stranger called back.

"Who?"

"Your neighbor, Arnold. I live just next door."

Scar looked out the window again to see if he could see anyone else. It looked to him like this dude was alone, and he for sure looked harmless. After contemplating a moment, Scar figured it was safe to open the door.

"Hello," said Arnold as the door opened to reveal Scar.

"What's up?" Scar replied to the white man wearing a wide-brimmed straw hat and overalls.

"I just came over to say hello and welcome you to our community," Arnold said. His warm smile formed his thin face into something out of a Norman Rockwell painting.

Scar was caught off guard by this unsolicited kindness. A neighbor coming over to introduce himself would never happen in the hood.

"Oh. Word. That's cool."

"I brought you some vegetables from my garden. May I come in?" Before Scar could react, Arnold had handed him a wicker basket and walked into the house.

"I thought they would never sell this place. It's been vacant ever since Miss Sally passed away. Going on two years now. Oh well, guess that's the recession they are always going on about on the TV. I like what you've done with the place." Arnold slowly walked around the living room.

"Yeah, well, I was just gettin' ready to leave. So, nice meeting you." Scar was finally able to compose himself and say something.

"Oh, right. Of course. I'm so rude. I just got so excited when I saw that someone finally moved in, I had to come over. I love having neighbors. I think of them as my family. Are you here alone?"

"Yeah, it's just me." Scar looked at the door, wishing this dude would walk through it and leave.

"Oh, well, you'll have to come over for dinner. I'm just over the other side of the tree line there." He pointed to the east side of the house, where the trees were the thickest.

"Yeah, maybe."

"I get it. You're shy. Well, I won't bite. My wife and I own a small farm over there. Nothing fancy, just enough to get by. We don't need much to be happy when we have each other." Arnold smiled.

"Uh-huh." Scar awkwardly smiled back. *What the fuck is this cracker talking about?* he thought.

"You should stop by the farmers' market this weekend. I sell my vegetables there on Saturdays and Sundays. It'd be a great way to get to know everyone in the community."

"Yeah, we'll see. I really gotta be going."

"Oh, right. I forgot. I'm sorry."

Just as Arnold was starting to leave, Scar's niece and nephew came into the living room. Arnold stopped abruptly.

"Uncle Scar, there's a bunch of dead birds in the yard. Did the fireworks kill them?" his niece said.

"Yeah, little one, that's what happened. Now, go on back outside and play. Take these vegetables to the kitchen." He handed her the basket.

"Where did you get these?"

"This nice man." Scar gestured to Arnold, who had a confused look on his face. When he realized he was being talked about, Arnold reacted like he had been thinking about something else.

"Huh? Oh, yes. Those are from my garden. Enjoy." Arnold smiled at the little girl and boy.

"Thanks." They walked off, examining the vegetables.

Scar looked at Arnold to gauge his reaction to seeing the kids. His face seemed expressionless. Scar always had trouble reading white people. They all seemed the same to him.

The kids had been on the news as missing, so Scar needed to know if Arnold had recognized them. He couldn't just outright ask him.

Scar said the first thing that popped into his head. "They came to visit and see my new place. Get out of the city for a few days."

"Sure. Right. That's what I heard this morning. Fireworks. Funny, I thought it might be gunshots or something. Oh well, I've taken up enough of your time." Arnold briskly walked out the front door.

Little did Scar know, Arnold had come over because he had heard the gunshots and he came to investigate. Arnold hated guns; they actually scared him.

Scar was shocked. He didn't know what to do. Did Arnold recognize his niece and nephew? Did he recognize Scar? Why did he seem so strange after the kids came in the house? There were too many unanswered questions for Scar's liking.

He decided he needed to stop Arnold before he alerted the cops. He pulled his gun out of his waistband and went out the front door. The second he got past the threshold, he ran right into Flex.

"Ay, yo. Where you goin' in such a rush, nigga?" Flex said.

"Kill my country-ass neighbor."

"Who? That cracker I saw just walk in them woods?"

"Yeah, him. He already in the woods? Fuck." Scar thought about chasing him, but decided it might be best not to kill him. He figured dude's wife probably knew where he was going and would come looking for him if he didn't come back. Scar would just have to be on high alert from now on.

"You want me to take care of it, boss?" Flex reached for the gun in his coat pocket.

"Nah. Leave it. We just need to be on guard. Matter of fact, get a nigga in here to install a security system. See if any mu'fuckin' police tryin'a creep up on us."

"Bet." Flex entered the house.

Scar looked toward the woods before he re-entered the house. *Damn. I thought it would be peaceful up in the country. Nigga can't get away from stress anywhere.*

Chapter 2

Powdered Courage

Security was tight at the funeral for former Chief of Staff Dexter Coram. The procession of politicians from the city and state seemed endless—not because they liked Dexter and wanted to pay their respects, but because every press outlet was there and they could get their faces on TV and their names in the papers. In fact, most of them were grossed out by Dexter and his sleazy, down-low, perverted flirting. If they didn't think they could promote their agendas, they wouldn't have been there.

Lurking just on the outskirts of the funeral was Dexter's boss, Mathias Steele. The disgraced former mayor was not invited to the funeral. Most of the city was blaming him for the death of Dexter Coram, as well as for the corruption that had riddled the city of Baltimore during his tenure as mayor. Many people in his government had been killed, including three police chiefs and most every member of the drug task force, the D.E.S. The only surviving member of the D.E.S was Derek Fuller, who happened to be the brother of Scar Johnson, the most notorious gangster in Baltimore.

"Look at these hypocritical sons of bitches," Mathias snarled as he watched the politicians enter the church. The park across the street from the church created a nice vantage point for him to watch without being seen or recognized. "Not one of those cocksuckers is clean, and they all turned their backs on me." Mathias was enraged and mumbling to himself like a homeless person.

The minute word had gotten out that the governor was forcing Mathias to step down as mayor, no one would return his phone calls. All of his once-allies were now his enemies, and he was hell bent on making them pay for their disloyalty.

"You'll get yours, you bastards. I'll make sure of it. First I'll take out Scar Johnson, and then y'all are next." He took mental notes of every politician who entered the church.

As the crowd out in front of the church was dwindling and the funeral seemingly about to start, the biggest motorcade of them all came rolling in. From the limousine stepped Governor Thomas Tillingham. Mathias's blood boiled at the sight of the governor. He was the one man Mathias had needed to stand behind him, but the governor was the first to turn his back. Even as the mayor had struggled to keep morale high in the city, his approval rating was dropping. Residents were losing faith. When Police Chief Hill and Dexter Coram were blown up separately on the same day, the city was suddenly on a witch hunt, and Mathias was the target. When the governor came in, he could have backed Mathias and calmed the cries for his resignation, but instead the governor forced him out of office. It was politics as usual. In the end, no one had any loyalty.

Mathias watched the governor shake a few hands and make his presence known before entering the church. The hoopla died down and calm descended upon the

street. The only people left were the press and State
Police keeping an eye on the surrounding area. Calm-
ing himself down, Mathias sat on a bench and read the
newspaper he had bought on his way to the funeral.

His calm didn't last for long. The headline that he
had been avoiding since he bought the paper brought
his anger right back. It read: HOW MUCH DID HE STEELE?
The article was full of speculation about Mathias and
his time as mayor. Mathias was furious about the
things being said about him in the article. He was being blamed for the crime on the streets and for allowing
Scar free reign over the poorest neighborhoods while
protecting the rich sections. The article blamed him for
starting a class war and turning his back on the needi-
est citizens. They also hinted that he may have actually
been working with Scar.

The thing that really upset Mathias the most was
the part of the article that said the governor had come
in and rescued Baltimore. Officially the deputy mayor
was in charge, but everyone in politics knew that Governor Tillingham had taken control and was cleaning
up the corruption left behind by Mathias Steele. Mathias felt like the article made him look incompetent as it
blamed him for all of the city's problems.

Mathias was in denial and blamed Scar for the problems in the city. "I'm gonna clear my name and show
these fuckers who's really responsible for this shit."

Mathias closed the newspaper and turned his eyes
to the front of the church. After an hour of sitting there
and obsessing over the article, he watched the people
file out at the end of the funeral service. Governor Tillingham appeared at the top of the steps and the media
swarmed. The governor held court like a king among
his peasants. Mathias seethed on the inside.

As the governor was speaking to the press, he looked across the street into the park. Without missing a beat, he whispered into the ear of one of his staff, who then whispered into the ear of one of the police officers guarding him. The next thing Mathias knew, there was an officer standing right next to him.

"Sir, I am going to have to ask you to leave," the officer said to Mathias.

"This is a public park. I think I'll stay," Mathias calmly replied without looking at him.

"Sir, I don't want to ask you again. You need to leave this area. It's for security purposes," he said a little more forcefully.

"I am no threat, and you can't make me leave a public space. Now I'm asking you to leave," Mathias replied, keeping his eyes locked on Governor Tillingham.

The governor was watching the whole thing transpire while he kept answering questions from the press.

The officer quietly spoke into the microphone attached to the sleeve of his suit, then awaited the reply from his superior. "Copy," the officer answered.

"Sir, if you do not cooperate, I will have no choice but to use force to remove you."

"Fuck you." Mathias lost his cool. "Do you know who I am? I'm the mayor of Baltimore. You take orders from me." Mathias was staring at his reflection in the cop's sunglasses.

The officer grabbed Mathias by the arm with one hand, while his other hand was on his weapon. He picked Mathias up off the bench and began shoving him away from the church.

"If you don't leave now, I'll arrest you."

"Fuck you. I'm the mayor!"

"No, sir, you were the mayor. Now you are no one." The cop pushed Mathias to the ground.

Mathias was humiliated and wanted to jump up and fight. He thought better of it when he looked up at the officer standing over him with his weapon drawn.

"You'll regret this." Mathias stood up covered in dirt and walked away steaming mad.

It was now a tie between Scar and the governor at the top of Mathias's most hated list. As he walked away, Mathias vowed to himself to give a little payback to the governor for his disrespect.

Mathias walked into East Baltimore with one thing on his mind. He needed to buy a gun. He didn't know how to go about buying one, but he figured he had a good chance of buying it in the hood. As mayor, he spent no time in these neighborhoods. This was all new territory to him. He felt like an exposed target walking these streets. His designer suit and tie made him stick out like a sore thumb.

He tried to appear calm as he proceeded down Eastern Avenue. His eyes were darting back and forth; his body was tense, like he was waiting for an attack at any minute.

A young boy about thirteen years old jumped out of a doorway and blocked Mathias from going any farther. "The fuck you doin' around here, nigga?" the boy asked.

"I'm looking to purchase something," Mathias said.

"You got money, I got what you need. I can make you feel good."

"I'm not here to buy drugs."

"The fuck you need then?"

"Young man, I doubt you can help me. I need to speak with someone older. Perhaps you have an older brother?" Mathias asked.

The young banger looked at Mathias with disgust and confusion on his face. They stood staring at each other, the boy trying to figure this dude out, and Mathias not knowing what to do or how these negotiations were supposed to happen.

"Yeah, a'ight. I can introduce you to my brother. He inside. Follow me."

They walked toward the boarded up house they had been standing in front of. The boy walked up the three steps to the front door and pushed the plywood board back so they could enter. As soon as Mathias was inside the doorway, the young boy spun around and caught him with a fist to his jaw, sending Mathias slamming into the wall.

"Mu'fucka, who you think you is? I got what you need." The boy stood in front of Mathias, pointing a gun at him.

Mathias was stunned.

"Now, what you need, nigga?"

"I—I need a gun," Mathias stammered. His heart was racing. Never before had he been in a situation where his life could end at any second. He had been sheltered his whole life. He was now getting a taste of what the streets were really like.

"Shit. Why you think I can't get that for you?"

"I don't know. I've never bought a gun before."

"You a cop?" the kid asked.

"No."

"You look like a cop. I hate cops. I have no problem shooting cops."

"I'm not, I'm not. I swear." Mathias was trembling.

The boy stood there studying Mathias. He wasn't nervous at all, because he had been on the streets since he was nine. He'd lost any fear he had years ago.

"Open yo' shirt."

"What?"

"Open yo' shirt. I wanna see if you wired."

"What?"

The boy reached out and ripped open Mathias's shirt, exposing his bare chest. "A'ight, you ain't wired. Step into my home." The boy pushed Mathias deeper inside the house and followed behind, keeping his gun aimed at Mathias's back.

The house was dark and cold. There was no furniture except for a television, a dirty mattress on the floor, and an old torn-up couch in the living room. The boy pushed Mathias down onto the couch. Mathias was beginning to think his life was going to end in this god-forsaken place.

The boy pulled a pen cap out of his pocket, along with a baggie full of cocaine, and tossed both to Mathias. "Yo, before we go any further, you need to take a bump from that baggie."

Mathias caught the baggie and pen cap. "I don't know what that means."

"Nigga, snort some cocaine from the bag so I know you legit. Scoop it out with the pen cap and snort it."

"I'm not here to buy drugs."

"Mu'fucka, if you don't snort some shit right now, you gonna die." He raised the gun and aimed it a Mathias's head.

"Okay, okay." Mathias opened the bag, scooped out a huge bump, and snorted it up his left nostril. He immediately felt a burning, then a numbing sensation in his nostril. To him it felt like the cocaine shot straight through his skull, directly into his brain. His eyes widened and his heart started racing. He felt great.

"Wow!" Mathias smiled, which made the boy smile as well.

"Now I know you legit. You want a gun? You wanna be a gangbanger, Grandpa?"

"Yeah, I need a gun." The cocaine was making Mathias clench his jaw.

"A'ight. I can get you a gun. But you ain't just buying a gun from me. I'm a businessman, and my business is cocaine. You need to buy some shit from me so my bosses can see I'm hustlin' out here."

"Oh, definitely. Whatever you need." Mathias's leg was twitching rapid fire.

"How much money you got?"

"I have a thousand dollars. Is that enough?"

The boy didn't say anything. He just stared at Mathias. This was much more than the boy was going to ask for. He was trying to hide his shock and excitement.

"Damn. That's all you have? Usually I wouldn't do this, but I like you, so I'll sell you a gun and that bag for a thousand. You gettin' a good deal. Normally it would be at least fifteen hun'ed."

"Thanks. I appreciate it." Thoughts were racing through Mathias's mind a mile a minute. He reached in his pocket and handed the boy the stack of cash.

"Bullets not included." The boy emptied the clip of his gun and handed it to Mathias.

"Oh, sure. Yeah, of course." Mathias put the gun in his pocket. Now that their transaction was complete, both of them couldn't wait to leave. The boy wanted to jet before this dude realized he got suckered. Mathias wanted to leave because the cocaine had him so high he needed to get outside and walk.

"You need more coke, you come see me. I got rock, too, if you need it," the boy said.

"Yeah, yeah, okay." Mathias walked out as fast as he could.

Once on the street, Mathias was so high he didn't realize that he speed-walked all the way back to his nice, safe section of Baltimore. The cocaine had him flying high and feeling like he could conquer the world. He was positive that he would destroy Scar and Governor Tillingham now that he had a gun. He felt invincible, and he couldn't wait to get home to do another bump of coke.

Chapter 3

Hotel Love

The lobby of the downtown Baltimore hotel was empty as Cecil entered through the front door. He wasn't surprised, since it was the middle of the night. He saw only one person, a little Asian man swinging a buffing machine back and forth over the marble floor.

I don't know why motherfuckers don't be robbin' hotels more often. Ain't no one here to stop you. I might have to take this place down myself, he thought.

He made his way through the massive lobby to the front desk. Sitting atop the counter was a silver bell like Cecil had seen in the movies.

This shit is crazy. Not even a person at the front desk. I should just rob this place now and stay somewhere else.

He pushed the button to ring the bell. There was some rustling in the office to the left behind the desk. After a short delay, a young white guy in his early twenties came out of the office. His eyes were bloodshot and his hair was disheveled. Cecil figured the kid had been asleep in the office.

"Hello, sir. How can I help you?" the clerk said.

"I need a room."

"All right." The clerk typed something on the keyboard and read the computer screen in front of him. "Do you have a reservation?"

"No, I don't. I didn't think I would need one." Cecil joked, "And by the looks of your empty lobby, don't look like I need one."

Either the clerk didn't get the joke or he ignored it. "Okay, sir. No problem. I would be glad to assist you." He typed a few more things into the computer. "Will you be needing one or two beds?"

"One."

"We have a nice deluxe room with a king size bed."

"That sounds fine."

"I'll just need some information from you. First and last name, please."

Cecil was a little caught off guard by the question. He paused for a second. He knew enough not to give his real name. "Chuck Bell."

"Okay, Mr. Bell. Your mailing address?"

"Ah, well, that's a problem." Cecil paused and the clerk looked up from the computer screen. "See, my wife and I are moving here to Baltimore, and we don't have a place to live yet. I just got a job. I had to leave Atlanta to move here."

He was lying, of course. He had come from Florida to Baltimore with Tiphani Fuller, his girlfriend. She had told him a sob story about how three men—Scar Johnson, Derek Fuller, and Mayor Mathias Steele— had ruined her life and taken advantage of her. She was seeking revenge against these three men and had convinced Cecil to help her kill them.

According to Tiphani, Scar was a vicious criminal who tried to have her killed after she presided over his case. Instead of protecting her, the mayor had Tiphani arrested for corruption, which Tiphani said was based on lies and rumors; and Derek was trying to keep Tiphani away from her children. For these actions, Tiphani decided they all needed to die, and Cecil was so blinded by the good head she gave him that he was willing to do anything for her.

Little did Cecil know that she had chosen him when she read his rap sheet while he was in prison. She saw that he was a decorated soldier with extensive combat experience. He was smart and dangerous, the perfect man for Tiphani's scheme. That was why she started visiting him in jail and developed a relationship that continued after he was released.

The clerk blankly looked at Cecil. Cecil had no idea what the kid was thinking, and it made him a little nervous. He quickly calmed down, telling himself there was no reason to worry. Tiphani was the only one who knew anything about his involvement in the recent murders in Baltimore, and she was an accomplice, so she sure as hell wasn't going to speak up. Cecil had made sure that a few weeks ago, when he came up from Florida for the first time, no one had seen him blow up the cars of Police Chief Hill and Chief of Staff Dexter Coram. Those murders were the first wave in Tiphani's retaliation, and they had brought about the firing of Mayor Steele. Now Tiphani and Cecil were here together to finish the job.

"Congratulations on your job, sir," the clerk said. "It's not a problem if you don't have an address. Your work address will be fine."

Damn. I can't tell him my job is to kill three dudes, Cecil thought.

"Ah, just put down City Hall as my workplace." It was the first place that came to Cecil's mind.

"Excellent, sir. You're here to get Baltimore back on the right track. Lots of changes going on over there at City Hall. Personally I thought Mayor Steele was horrible. I'm glad to see he's out of there." The clerk entered the address of City Hall without even needing to ask.

"Yeah, he made a real mess of this city. Unfortunate that the police chief and his chief of staff were murdered."

"Yes, it was. I hope they find the son of a bitch that did it. Excuse my language, sir. I just get angry when I think of innocent people losing their lives."

"It's all right. I like your passion. I hope they find him too." Cecil smiled. He found it funny that this kid had no clue he was speaking to the killer himself.

"Now, the last little part of business. I need a credit card from you."

"I'll be paying cash." Cecil started to take out a stack of bills from his pocket.

"That's fine, sir, but we still need a credit card for incidentals."

"I can pay cash for whatever that is," Cecil said.

"We need a credit card in case of damage to the room, and items from the mini-bar."

"I don't have my wallet. Just take the cash and I can get you the credit card tomorrow."

"I'm sorry," the clerk said. "That's not possible."

The clerk was starting to get on Cecil's nerves. Cecil didn't want to have to kill the kid, but if he started to feel like he was making too much of an impression on the kid and the clerk would remember him, then Cecil wouldn't hesitate to murder the little shit.

Cecil calmed himself down. "Okay, I understand," he said.

"Thank you. I'll be glad to give you a room once you have your credit card, Mr. Bell," the clerk responded.

Cecil walked away boiling on the inside. He had wanted to stay at a "no-tell motel," but Tiphani insisted on staying at a 5-star hotel. Ever since he had met her in Florida, Tiphani had been a bit too reckless for Cecil's liking. She was supposed to be hiding out down there, but she would often go out without any sort of disguise and spend large amounts of money on frivolous things. This type of thing was exactly what he wanted to avoid.

Cecil walked outside to the car, where Tiphani was waiting. He got back into the driver's seat.

"So? We checked in?" she asked.

"No, the little fucker needed a credit card and wouldn't let it slide. I told you we needed to go to one of them hourly joints. They don't be asking all sorts of questions like this bougie-ass place." Cecil put the keys in the ignition to drive off.

"Hold on. We ain't goin' to no sleazy hooker hotel. Do I gotta do everything?" Tiphani pulled the visor down, checked herself in the mirror, applied lipstick, and straightened her wig. "Give me the cash. I'll be back with a room key."

Cecil handed her the cash, and she stepped out of the car and strutted into the hotel. She was sick of all these trifling men in her life letting her down. It always seemed like she had to do everything. Every man she came into contact with tried to play her, and now she was going to play them. It was her time. These men could all go to hell, and she was going to be the one to send them there.

Just as Cecil did, Tiphani rang the bell that sat on top of the front desk. The young clerk appeared a moment later.

"May I help you?" the clerk began.

"Hello. My husband was just in here, and there seems to be a misunderstanding."

"You must be Mrs. Bell." The clerk smiled.

"Ah, yes, yes, I'm Mrs. Bell." Tiphani quickly realized that Cecil must have given a fake name.

"Welcome. As I explained to your husband, our policy is that we need a credit card to reserve a room."

"But we would like to pay cash. We hate those damn extra fees the credit cards charge."

"I hear you. Those interest rates will kill you. These days you got to save any way you can."

"I'm glad we cleared that up. So, how much is the room? We'll pay for the whole week up front." Tiphani went into her purse to get the cash.

"Oh, no. You misunderstand me. You can pay cash at the end of your stay. We need a credit card at the beginning to safeguard against anyone running out on the bill and to cover any extra charges that may occur."

"I can assure you we won't run out on no bill. We're not some ghetto couple," she said.

"Yes, I understand your husband works for City Hall."

Tiphani was taken aback for a second. *What the fuck this nigga been telling this boy?* she thought. Then, just as fast, she got amused by the irony and humor in the fact that Cecil said he worked for City Hall, since he had already killed the chief of staff and was back again to kill the former mayor.

"Yes, he does. We are very excited to be here with all of the changes. Any idea what happened to Mayor Steele?"

"No, ma'am. The news is saying he walked out of his office and hasn't been heard from since. Good riddance, I say. He was the worst."

Tiphani giggled. "Yes, he was." She was hoping that their mutual dislike for Mathias Steele would make the clerk bend the rules and let them stay without giving a credit card.

The clerk smiled at Tiphani. "I like you guys. So many times guests come in here and are so rude when I tell them they need a credit card."

"I like you too. You're cute. I promise we won't ruin your room."

"I know you won't, but I still need a card. If it was up to me, I'd let you stay, but it's not. I'm trying to put myself through college with this job. I don't need to be getting fired right now." He shrugged his shoulders.

"That is so commendable that you are putting yourself through college. I did the same thing."

"So you understand."

"I do. Do you know what I did to put myself through college . . ."—she looked at his nametag—"Evan?" She said his name seductively. She was done trying to get what she wanted through normal means. She was going to plan B. She was going to get what she wanted from a man the easiest way she knew how. Tiphani found that men were always willing to barter when sex was involved.

"No, ma'am, I don't." He was a little uncomfortable all of a sudden.

"Well, let's just say that if I can show you, I can promise you would be satisfied."

"Ma'am?"

"Is there anyone back there with you?" Tiphani asked, looking toward the office.

"No."

She leaned over the desk and whispered in his ear. "Then let me come back there. I want to taste you."

Evan's dick sprang to attention. He stood there frozen, unable to move. He had spent many late nights fantasizing that a guest would come down and offer herself to him. Now that it was happening, he didn't know how to react.

"Come on, baby. Open the door." Tiphani seductively massaged her breasts.

Evan swallowed hard. His heart was beating fast. He went around and opened up the door to the back office. Tiphani came around and followed Evan into the office.

"Now, I'll give you what you want, and I promise it will be the best you have ever had. You need to promise to give me what I want."

"Mrs. Bell, I can't. I'll lose my job."

Tiphani reached down, undid his belt, and unzipped his pants. Evan sucked in a deep breath of air. His legs began to tremble; he was so excited and nervous.

Tiphani got on her knees and pulled out his dick. She was excited as well. She thought of white boys' dicks as a treat, like a kind of dessert. She always thought that white boys were juicy and loved their taste. She was pleased with the size when she unleashed his manhood and began kissing the head.

"Now"— she gave a little kiss—"how about"—another kiss—"you let me"— another kiss—"pay cash?" Another kiss, then she looked into Evan's eyes before swallowing his entire dick in one gulp.

"Ahhh. Okay!" Evan groaned.

Tiphani began sliding her mouth up and down on his shaft. Evan tilted his head back and closed his eyes in ecstasy. He couldn't believe what was happening.

Tiphani stroked and sucked his dick furiously. She was loving the taste of this young college white boy. "Mmmmmm. I love this dick," she moaned as she continued stroking his shaft with her left hand and playing with her clit with the right. She then started sucking on his balls. This drove Evan over the edge.

"Oh God. That is good. Oh shit." He looked down to watch Tiphani work.

He grabbed her head and forced his dick into her mouth again. She took it with ease as he began fucking her face. He gave her mouth full strokes, and her saliva acted as lubrication. He had never had a woman be able to swallow his whole dick.

He got so turned on watching his cock pump in and out of her face that he couldn't take it anymore. He pulled out and shot his load all over her face, just like he had seen in the many pornos he watched late at night at work.

He stood there panting and smiling as he watched Tiphani wipe cum from her cheeks and lips. "Mm-mmm." She licked her fingers.

"Holy shit. I feel like I was in a porno. That was amazing." He put his dick back in his pants and zipped up.

Tiphani got back to her feet. "So, will I be staying in your hotel?" She smirked.

"I'll see what I can do." Evan smirked back.

A short while later, Tiphani walked back outside to the car. She knocked on the driver's side window, startling Cecil awake. He jumped, wiped his eyes, and opened the window.

"Room sixteen-oh-four. Bring the bags up." She handed him a room key and walked back into the hotel.

She went back to the desk one more time and rang the bell. Evan appeared, still looking a little flustered.

"Hey." He had a huge smile on his face when he saw Tiphani.

"Here's a little extra for your college fund." She winked, handed him five hundred dollars, and walked to the elevators. Evan stood there shocked and in love as he watched her get in the elevator.

Tiphani was in the shower when Cecil entered the room. She finished washing up, dried off, and hopped in bed, where Cecil was already under the covers, watching television.

"What did you do to get this room?" he asked.

"Something you couldn't, obviously." She pulled the blanket up to her neck.

"What would that be?"

"I charmed him and helped him relieve some stress."

"What's that supposed to mean?"

"Exactly what it sounds like. I got down on his level and told him how I put myself through college."

"How did you do that?"

"I fucked dudes for cash." She turned her back on Cecil.

"Baby, that is so sexy." He nestled up behind her and pressed his dick into her ass cheeks.

"I'm not fucking you right now," she said.

"Come on, baby. That story made me horny." His dick started to get hard as he rubbed it on her ass.

"I want to sleep. Tomorrow we start our hunt for the three dead men." She was using the nickname they had come up with for Scar, Derek, and Mathias.

"Come on." He reached around and started playing with Tiphani's pussy.

It turned her on. Cecil's fingers made her realize she didn't get off when she sucked Evan, and her pussy needed some attention. She started to breathe heavier and opened her legs a bit for easier access.

"I promise tomorrow I will hit the streets hard looking for them mu'fuckas," Cecil whispered in her ear.

Without saying anything, Tiphani guided Cecil's dick inside her, and he started fucking her from behind.

Chapter 4

Fight for My Life

"Let me the fuck out of here!" Halleigh screamed at the top of her lungs. Her muscles ached, her throat hurt, and her eyes were stinging from crying. She was locked in a small room with a single mattress. There was a tiny bathroom attached with a sink and toilet. She had no idea how she had gotten there. The last thing she remembered before waking up was being in the trunk of a car.

Former detective Derek Fuller had kidnapped Halleigh because he was desperate to get his kids back from Scar. He knew that Halleigh's boyfriend, Day, worked for Scar. Derek kidnapped Halleigh and told Day that if he wanted her back, he would have to get Derek's kids from Scar. So far it wasn't working. Day claimed he didn't even know where Scar went after he escaped from the city. Derek didn't give a shit what Day said; he was going to hold Halleigh until he got his kids back.

Because of the lack of windows in the room, Halleigh had no concept of time and no idea how long she had been there. To Halleigh, it felt like an eternity. She was slowly beginning to lose her will to live. Her life was a constant struggle, and she was tired of the fight. She felt like she was never able to catch a break. Whenever she felt like she was on the right track, someone would come along and put an end to her peaceful feeling. This time, that person was Derek Fuller.

The lock on the door unlatched. The loud thud startled Halleigh and made her jump. She was definitely on edge. Derek Fuller violently pushed the door open and entered.

"The fuck you screaming for again?" he said.

"Fuck you!" she spat.

"I told you no one can hear you and I don't give a fuck."

Halleigh had nothing to say to that. She stared at Derek, wishing he would die. She felt powerless. She was unable to do anything and started to cry.

"Goddamn." Derek walked out and locked the door behind him.

Halleigh collapsed on top of the mattress, sobbing. She wished her life would end. Lying there she thought back on her life—raped as a young girl, forced into prostitution, her first true love murdered. She realized that she was never in control of any of it. She was always a victim; someone else always dictated what path her life would take. Then she started to think about her little boy, the love of her life, the only one that mattered to her. She saw his smiling face, she heard his laugh. The vision strengthened her and stopped her sobbing. Halleigh didn't want her son raised without his mother. She needed to protect him and teach him how to be strong.

How can I teach my boy to be strong if I can't show him a good example and be strong myself? she thought. She resolved right there to stop being a victim, to start taking matters into her own hands and dictate how her life would go from that point on. She was doing it for her son. Malek Jr. was going to be a survivor, and Halleigh was going to teach him how.

Sitting up, she tried to come up with a plan to escape. She took a mental inventory of the room. The only thing there was the mattress she was currently sitting on and a fluorescent light recessed into the ceiling. In the bathroom was a bar of soap, a toothbrush, and toothpaste. She saw nothing that could help her. The only way out she saw was going to be to fight. If she could take Derek by surprise, she might have a chance to stun him long enough to escape.

Halleigh went to the door and stood in different positions around it, seeing which one might be the most advantageous for her attack. None seemed particularly good. She looked around the room once more. Pretending to be asleep when he came in was out of the question. She figured being in a prone position would put her at a disadvantage and weaken her. There didn't seem to be any good place in the room to take Derek by surprise.

Halleigh then had the thought that she would hide in the bathroom. When he entered, she would wait until he was in front of the bathroom door, and then rush out and attack him, possibly hitting him with the door and knocking him out. This was her best chance, she thought.

Halleigh waited in the bathroom for what seemed like an eternity. While sitting on the toilet, she thought about her son—his laugh, his smile, how he must be missing his mama. This gave her more motivation and energy for her attack.

Being confined in such a small space was making her antsy. Her nerves were making her rock back and forth, continuously sit up and then right back down, and pacing for two steps back and forth. She thought about screaming to get him down there faster but decided against it. She wanted him relaxed to catch him off guard. If she screamed, he would be coming down already on edge and looking for trouble.

Derek unlocked the door and entered holding a paper plate with a peanut butter and jelly sandwich. Halleigh held her breath when she heard the door open. Her heart was in her throat and her mouth went instantly dry. Now that the time had arrived for her to fight, she wasn't sure she could go through with it.

"Hey," Derek called out.

Halleigh didn't answer. She just stared at the door.

Derek stepped farther into the room. "Halleigh? I brought you food."

Again, no answer from Halleigh.

"You in the bathroom?" Derek walked toward the bathroom door.

Halleigh listened to his footsteps getting closer to the door. This was it, time for her to decide if she was going through with it. She stood up from the toilet and quietly placed her hand on the door handle. One half of her wanted to just open the door and take the food, and the other half was ready to fight. She was struggling with her emotions and was afraid to make a decision.

"Stop fuckin' around. You in there?" He raised his voice as he directed it toward the bathroom. He was standing directly in front of the bathroom door.

Decision time. Halleigh turned the knob and opened the door with all the force she could muster. "AGHH-HHH!" She screamed, slamming the door into Derek and knocking him back. The sandwich went flying to the floor.

Halleigh rushed out and jumped on top of Derek, raining punches down on him. Continuing to scream to keep her adrenaline up, she landed punches wherever she could and with as much force as possible.

Derek covered his face and tried to avoid the windmill of punches being thrown at him. After his initial shock was over, Derek realized that her punches weren't doing any harm. In one swift movement, he grabbed Halleigh's arms and flung her off of him, sending her crashing into the wall. She crumbled to the floor in a heap.

Derek immediately pounced on top of her and subdued her. He pinned her down on the floor, making it impossible for her to move. She struggled to get free, but his weight was too much for her. After several seconds of fighting to break free she gave up, but before she did, she spit in his face. It was the only thing she could do to feel as though she still had some power and to let him know how she felt about him.

"Fuck you, bitch. I ought to beat your ass," he said.

"Fuck you, motherfucker." She attempted to wriggle free.

"The fuck you thinkin'?"

"The fuck you think I'm thinkin'?" she shot back.

"You're a dumb ass tryin' to come at me like that." He laughed.

Her face was tight with anger and embarrassment. "Just get up off me."

"Nah. I kind of like being on top of you." Derek smirked and moved his hips in a sexual manner.

Halleigh was disgusted. She was mad at herself for trying to overpower Derek. She was mad for not thinking of a better way to escape.

"Fine. Stay on top of me. Do whatever you want to do," she said in a monotone and turned her head.

"Shit, I don't want to do anything to you when you say it so unsexy. I'm not a rapist."

"No, you're just a kidnapper."

Derek had a mind to slap the bitch. "If I let you up, don't try any bullshit. I'll knock you the fuck out. Got it?"

"Whatever. I don't need to be bit more than once to know it hurts. Just let me up."

Derek jumped to his feet and put some distance between them. He made sure to land standing between the door and Halleigh, in case she had any ideas of trying to run out. She slowly stood as she straightened her clothes and hair.

"Thank you," she said, trying to regain her composure.

"What the hell?"

"I'm being held against my will. What do you think?" she said sarcastically.

Halleigh was wishing he would just leave. She had some planning to do. She was going to escape from captivity and find her son.

"Don't get sassy, bitch. It'll get you nowhere," he warned. "It's a shame you had to get stupid today. I was going to let you upstairs to take a shower."

"Big deal." She flicked her wrist.

"I was looking forward to watching you wash that fine little body of yours." He looked her up and down.

"Your loss, not mine." She shrugged her shoulders. She was trying to act cool. Her insides were doing back flips, and she didn't want him to know how scared and angry she was.

"I would say your loss. I might have even joined you in that shower. Now you'll just have to eat alone." He gestured with his head to the sandwich on the floor.

"Nothing to drink?"

"Water from the tap, bitch."

His phone vibrated in his pocket. He took it out and looked at the caller ID. "It's your knight in shining armor," he said to Halleigh.

"Dayvid?" Her mood perked up.

"Maybe he's ready to do right by you."

He answered the call, "Speak." He walked out and locked the door behind him.

"Dayvid!" Halleigh screamed, hoping that Dayvid would hear her. She ran to the door and put her ear to it, hoping to hear their conversation, but Derek was already out of range.

She let out a deep sigh and went straight to the bathroom. She was a ball of nerves. Now that Derek was gone, she couldn't hold her emotions back. Knowing that Dayvid was on the phone put her over the edge. The second she was in the bathroom, she leaned over and grabbed the sink with both hands and broke down crying.

Now she had even more incentive to break free. Before she was determined for her son, but the way she felt when she knew Dayvid was on the phone told her she needed to do it for him as well. She was in love with the man and wanted to be his wife. She wanted him to be her son's father. She wanted to give him a child.

These feelings for Dayvid had only recently begun to stir in Halleigh. When she met Dayvid, she was dating Malek and Dayvid was his protégé. After Malek was killed, Halleigh and Dayvid started spending more time together. During this time, their feelings for one another had blossomed.

"Get it together." She looked up above the sink out of habit to see her reflection, but there was no mirror.

Derek had removed it so she couldn't use the glass as a weapon.

"Damnit," she mumbled to herself.

Halleigh wiped the tears from her face and resolved to fight some more. She stood in the bathroom thinking of a way, any way, to escape. She wracked her brain, but nothing was coming. The only thing she could do was replay her last failed attempt over and over.

"Think, Halleigh, think." Her eyes searched the tiny bathroom. "I need a weapon." Her eyes continued to dart back and forth. They landed on her toothbrush.

"Holy shit. The toothbrush. People make shanks out of those in prisons." She snatched the toothbrush off the sink and frantically searched her "cell" for a surface to sharpen the toothbrush handle. She had a renewed burst of hope and energy.

That burst didn't last very long as she realized there weren't really any good surfaces for her to sharpen the toothbrush. The linoleum in the bathroom, the carpeting in the main room, and the dry wall in both were lousy as sharpening tools.

Fuck it, she thought and started to vigorously rub the toothbrush on the carpet, praying to God that her new plan for escape would work.

Chapter 5

The Hunt with Some Extra Baggage

"Speak," Derek answered the phone.

"We need to meet," Dayvid said. On the other end of the line he heard a muffled female voice calling his name.

"Halleigh!" he screamed, hoping she would hear him.

"No use screaming, nigga. She ain't gonna hear you."

"Let me speak to her. You better not do nothin' to her," Dayvid warned.

"I'm not doin' nothin' to her that she don't want," Derek taunted.

"I'll kill you, nigga."

"Come on, stop the bullshit." Derek chuckled.

"I swear to God, nigga." Dayvid was furious.

"You just do what you need to do and she'll be fine. But hurry up. I think she's startin' to feel me." Derek couldn't help giving Dayvid shit.

"Fuck you!" Dayvid screamed at the top of his lungs.

His screaming startled Malek Jr., who had been sleeping in the backseat of Dayvid's car.

"Dayvid?" Malek wiped his eyes.

Dayid removed the phone from his ear and covered the mouthpiece so Derek couldn't hear. "Hey, little man," he whispered. "Everything fine. Go back to sleep."

"You screamed," Malek Jr. said.

Dayvid put the phone back to his ear.

"Who the fuck you talkin' to?" Derek asked.

"None of yo' business."

"Is that D.J.?" Derek thought he might have heard his son in the background.

Dayvid realized from the urgency in Derek's voice that he could use this to his advantage. "It was no one." Dayvid made sure it sounded like he was trying to cover up that it was D.J.

"Let me speak to him." Derek sounded desperate. "D.J.!" he screamed.

"No use screaming, nigga. He ain't gonna hear you." Dayvid repeated Derek's words exactly.

"Fuck you!" Derek yelled.

"Looks like the tables have turned, nigga." Dayvid laughed.

Derek was livid. He wanted to strangle Dayvid. It killed him that he felt powerless to protect his children and that he had no idea where they were.

"Listen to me and listen good. If there is any harm to my children, if you have my kids and haven't given them to me, I will kill your woman right now."

Dayvid had a decision to make. Should he call Derek's bluff and continue making him think he had his kids, or should he tell the truth and buy some time? Dayvid looked at M.J., who was looking out the window, quietly singing to himself. Dayvid couldn't risk losing Halleigh. He would never forgive himself if he was responsible for M.J. growing up without his mother. He also wasn't sure if he was capable of raising M.J. on his own. It had only been a week and he was already having trouble taking care of him.

"Relax, nigga. It ain't yo' kid. I promise. But let me tell you, if you do any harm to Halleigh, I will find yo' kids and dead them little shits. You hear me?"

Derek had no choice but to believe him. "Okay, okay. Just get me my kids." He hung up.

"I'm hungry," Malek Jr. announced from the back seat.

"A'ight, little man. We'll get you some food in a minute."

"Nooo, I'm hungry now. Nuggets."

"Chill! We have to buy them shits first." Dayvid immediately felt bad for snapping at Malek. He turned to look at Malek and apologize. Malek was just staring at him with a scared and shocked look on his face. Dayvid couldn't have felt any worse. He was on edge. Taking care of a child and figuring out his next move was becoming a problem.

"I'm sorry. Let's get some nuggets." Dayvid pulled out into traffic, heading for the nearest fast food joint.

Dayvid drove along not really paying attention to where he was going. He was thinking about how he was going to get Derek's kids away from Scar. Hell, the first thing he needed to do was find Scar. It had been a week and Dayvid had not spoken to or seen Scar. As soon as Dayvid saw that Scar's house had been raided, he called Scar, but Scar didn't answer. Dayvid had no idea if Scar had been picked up or just threw his phone away. He spent all week at Halleigh's house watching the news for any information on Scar. Nothing was said about an arrest, so he figured Scar must have gotten out before the raid.

Dayvid figured he'd give one more attempt to reach Scar on his phone, though he didn't have much hope that he would. Dayvid dialed the number. He was right;

the phone was not in service. He wasn't surprised. When he saw the raid, the first thing Dayvid had done was throw his own phone away.

After a week away from the streets, he had no idea what was going on. He figured things had quieted down enough that he could come back out from hiding at Halleigh's. He needed to find Scar, somehow convince him to let Derek's kids go, and save Halleigh. He had a feeling that time was starting to run out on Derek's patience. He figured Derek was searching for Scar as well, and if Derek found him first, that would spell the end for Halleigh. Dayvid had to act fast.

Dayvid headed toward his old corner. He would start his search there, trying to get information on what the hell was happening, and hopefully find out about Scar. He rolled through the hood and saw some familiar faces, but it seemed different to him. He couldn't tell if it really was different, or if the week away from the grind had made him see things in a new light.

Some of the young soldiers out there hustling saw his car as he pulled up to his old corner. They thought he was a customer and started strolling to his car.

"Is this nuggets?" Malek asked.

"Oh, no, little man. Soon. I just need to talk to my friends for a second." Dayvid had completely forgotten that Malek was in the car.

The corner boy walked up and nodded his head. "What's good?" he asked.

"You tell me. Been out for a minute," Day responded.

"Oh shit. I didn't recognize your ride. What's crackin', Day? It's been a second. Where you been?" He reached out and they bumped fists.

"Layin' low after I seen Scar's joint get raided. You heard from that nigga?"

"Nah. Rumors and shit, but ain't nothin' definite."
The corner boy shrugged his shoulders.

"Word. You got any paper for me?"

"Nah, B. Flex come by earlier and collect."

"Yeah? Where he at? I need to connect with that
nigga," Dayvid asked.

"I'on't know. He don't be sayin' much. Did ask about
you, though."

"What's he askin'?"

"Nothin'. Same shit. 'You seen Day?' That kinda shit.
I told him no. You want me to say somethin' to him if I
see him?" the boy asked.

"Let him know I stopped by. Tell him to holla at
me." Dayvid wrote his number on a piece of paper and
handed it to the boy.

"Bet." The boy took the paper, they slapped palms,
and he walked back to his spot on the corner.

Dayvid drove off wishing he had been able to get
more information from the kid. He wasn't surprised
that Flex wasn't saying much. He suspected that Scar
had ordered everyone to be tight-lipped right now. After the death of the police chief a week earlier, the cops
were knocking down doors all over Baltimore. The less
anyone knew about Scar, the safer he would be.

Dayvid needed to find Scar. What was his next move?
Flex would know where Scar was. His plan was to drive
around to all the spots he thought Flex might be. Even if
Flex wasn't there, Dayvid would leave word that he was
back on the block.

He was focused now. He made a mental list of all the
spots he needed to hit. His mood was high. He turned
the car stereo on and stepped on the gas, his sights set
on his first stop.

"My tummy hurts," Malek Jr. said.

Dayvid didn't respond. He couldn't hear him over the music.

"My tummy hurts. I'm hungry," Malek said a little louder.

Dayvid heard him this time. "What?"

"My tummy hurts. Nuggets." Malek pointed to the fast food joint they were passing.

"Shit," Dayvid mumbled. He had forgotten again that M.J was in the car. "Okay. Let's get nuggets."

Malek smiled as Dayvid turned the car around.

Goddamn, this kid is going to get in my way. How the fuck I'm gonna deal with him? Dayvid thought as he pulled into the parking lot of the restaurant. He loved Malek, but the kid was pissing him off at that moment. He needed to find the kid's mother, but he couldn't do it if the kid was always looking to eat or complaining about being bored. How could Dayvid take care of his business and the kid at the same time? He needed to figure it out soon or Halleigh might be dead.

Chapter 6

Typical Country Morning

Scar walked downstairs after a long, restful night of sleep. No birds waking him up this morning. He smiled and said to himself, "Guess them birds got the hint."

Usually he was the first one awake in the house, but he had slept so long that his niece and nephew were already in the kitchen eating breakfast.

"How'd y'all get that cereal?" he asked.

"I climbed up and got it," said his eight-year-old niece, Talisa.

"You crazy." Scar smiled. He was feeling good from being so well rested. It's amazing what one good night's sleep can do for a person. The day before, Scar was ready to take his chances, leave his country house, and go back to Baltimore. Now he was chillin'.

No need to rush back to the bullshit hustle. I can just chill here, outta the limelight for a minute, and make my money from a distance, he thought.

He sat down and poured himself a bowl of cereal. They all sat in silence, each in their own thoughts. Scar looked out the window at the sun beaming between the trees. Maybe he could get used to this country living. He had never taken the time to look at trees or nature while he was living in the city. He was starting to enjoy the slower pace.

The silence was broken by D.J. "Uncle Scar, it's boring here."

"Play with yo' toys," Scar answered.

"They're no fun."

"Yeah, I'm bored here too. When is Mama and Daddy coming back?" Talisa chimed in.

"Soon," Scar lied.

"We want to go home," Talisa said.

"You ain't," Scar snapped.

The children were startled by his abrupt answer. Scar instantly felt bad seeing the shock, confusion, and sadness on their faces. He changed his tone immediately.

"How 'bout Flex take you to the store? Buy you what you want," he said smoothly.

The children didn't answer. They just shrugged their shoulders in agreement. The rest of their meal was finished in silence.

Scar understood the children's feelings. It was slow in the country, especially since they couldn't really travel around. Scar couldn't leave his property, so when Flex wasn't there, that meant the kids had to stay there as well.

"We're finished. May we be excused?" Talisa asked.

"Yeah, go on." Scar stayed staring out the window as the children scurried to their room.

Scar was starting to really love his niece and nephew, but he didn't want to be dealing with them all the time. He had his own shit to deal with, and he didn't want to have to handle their bullshit as well. Scar needed to figure out a way to end all of this mess soon so he could figure out what to do with these kids. He had a feeling that these kids would be without parents by the time all was said and done.

Scar felt it was inevitable that he was going to have to kill his brother. As far as Tiphani was concerned, he wasn't sure if he would ever see her again. She may have skipped the country after news of their affair broke and her career as a judge was destroyed. If he did see her again, he would be killing her too. Thinking about his brother and his ex-lover made him seethe.

Scar picked up his phone. "Yo, when you stoppin' here?" he asked Flex.

"On my way. Be there in like forty-five." Flex merged onto the highway.

"I need to blow off some steam. Pick up that ho Charisma on your way."

"A'ight. Gonna take me longer to be there, though."

"Just do it. I need to bust a nut all over that bitch. Get my head straight. You feel me?"

"Word, I feel you." Flex hung up and exited at the next off-ramp.

Scar cleared the table and turned on the television. The news about his manhunt had slowly been decreasing. Scar knew this meant nothing. He had gotten word from some of his soldiers that they were still looking for him just as hard, even if the news wasn't picking it up. He flipped through the channels, never really staying on one station for very long. His mind was distracted with thoughts of his brother. He was hoping he wouldn't have to kill him, but he knew that the moment he kidnapped Derek's kids, he had crossed a line and it was all-out war.

A few hours passed with Scar wandering around the house and the children playing in their room or in the backyard. This seemed to be the routine they were falling into.

"We're hungry." Talisa came through the back door.

Scar was getting fed up with having to deal with the kids' neediness. He wanted to say "Get it yourself." Instead, he asked them what they wanted.

"Spaghetti." D.J. followed his sister into the house.

Scar held his tongue and just sighed as he went to the kitchen to start cooking. He would take the opportunity to make something for himself as well. He hadn't realized how hungry he was until the children said something. As he was pouring water into a pot, Flex came striding through the front door.

"Ay, yo," Flex called out.

The children went running to greet him. These days, anything different to break up the monotony of the day would excite them.

"We going to the store," D.J. said to Flex.

"Great," Flex said, not really paying attention to the little boy.

"Who are you?" Talisa asked the woman in skin-tight jeans, high heels, and a form-fitting top.

"My name's Charisma, dear. What's yours?" Charisma bent down to shake Talisa's hand.

"Talisa. You want to play with my dolls?"

"Not now, dear. How 'bout later?"

"I'll get some new ones at the store for us." Talisa stared at Charisma with adoration. She hadn't been around a female in a long time.

Flex and Charisma walked into the kitchen, where Scar had already dumped the water from the pot into the sink.

"Brought you some presents." Flex smiled and emptied a duffel bag full of cash onto the kitchen table. "Business startin'a pick up again."

"Okay, okay. My day is startin' to look up." Scar rubbed his hands together. He picked up some of the bills to see what denomination they were. Looked like mostly fifties and hundreds to Scar. He put the money back in the pile.

"What's good, ma? Come here and give yo' man some love," Scar said to Charisma. She seductively walked over to Scar, wrapped her arms around his neck, and began kissing him. Scar grabbed her ass as they kissed and grinded their pelvises into one another. Scar's dick was standing at attention. He broke their embrace.

"Get yo' ass upstairs and be ready for me," he said to her.

She composed herself, straightened her hair, and walked out of the room without saying a word.

"While I take care of my business upstairs, take them kids to the store and buy them whatever they want. They buggin' me with their whining and shit, sayin' they bored." Scar reached into the pile of cash and handed a fistful of bills to Flex. "This should cover it. If not, fuck 'em. Oh, get 'em some food too." He handed him a hundred dollar bill from the pile.

"D.J, Talisa, let's go," Flex called out.

The kids came running into the kitchen ready to head out the door. The minute Flex walked through the door, they had been prepared to leave. They couldn't wait to get out of the house. Flex gathered them up and followed them out the front door.

Scar quickly got to his bedroom, where Charisma was already making herself comfortable on the bed.

"Your kids is cute," Charisma said.

"They my niece and nephew. Why you ain't naked yet?" Scar asked.

"It's more fun when you take my clothes off for me," she purred.

"A'ight." Scar approached the bed, his smile broken up by the namesake scar that disfigured his face. He eased her back and lay on top of her. They started right where they had left off in the kitchen, grinding their pelvises and passionately kissing. Scar removed her top to reveal perfect, firm breasts, and started sucking her nipples.

"Mmmm. Yeah, Daddy," she cooed. She reached down to unleash his manhood.

She stroked his erection. "Oh, Daddy, I want to give you your own baby. Fill me up. I'll be your baby mama."

Scar jerked back from her. "The fuck you just say?"

"Nothin'. I don't know. I was just talkin' dirty." She tried to kiss him.

"Like hell you was talkin' dirty."

"Baby, come on. Make my pussy hurt. I need it." She reached down for his dick.

"You tryin'a trap a nigga'? I oughta beat yo' ass for thinkin' that shit." Scar was getting progressively angrier.

Just as he was about to haul off and hit Charisma to knock some sense into the bitch, there was a knock at the front door.

"Who the fuck?" Scar jumped to his feet and grabbed a gun from under his bed. As quietly as possible, he walked downstairs to the front door. There was another knock on the door, and then the doorbell rang. Scar cocked his gun. He couldn't think of who could be at his door.

Goddamn, we need to get a security system up in here. Scar walked to the window in order to catch a glimpse of the motherfucker who was knocking on his door. As he peeked out the window, he looked directly into the eyes of his neighbor. Arnold waved when he saw Scar looking out the window.

"Hello, neighbor," Arnold called out.

Fuck. He saw me. Why this white mu'fucka keep bothering me?

Scar begrudgingly opened the front door. "You need something?" he asked.

"Oh, no. Just stopping over to say hello. Cooking up some oxtails later. Trying something new to expand my palette. Wanted to invite you and the kids over for a little feast."

"No. Can't make it."

"Oh, come on. It'll be fun. A little getting to know your neighbors session."

"Don't think the kids like oxtail."

"No worries. I can make them some grilled cheese sandwiches or whatever they prefer."

"Maybe another night."

"Oh, nonsense. I won't take no for an answer. Let's say seven o'clock?"

"Um . . ." Scar didn't trust this cat. He wasn't buying this neighborly crap. There was some other reason this dude kept coming around. But just in case this dude was legit, Scar played it cool.

"Great," Arnold said, not even waiting for an answer. "Seven o'clock. Say, before I get out of your hair, do you mind if I use your commode?"

"What?"

"Your bathroom. Do you mind if I use it? I don't think I'll be able to hold it in until I get through the woods to my home. Weak bladder." In an attempt to make a joke, Arnold made a grimacing facial expression.

Scar sighed in exasperation. "Fine. Make it fast." He stepped aside to let Arnold in.

"It's around the corner." Scar pointed in the direction of the bathroom.

Scar anxiously waited at the front door for Arnold to do his business.

Charisma came down from the bedroom. "Come back to bed, Daddy," she said seductively.

"Get yo' ass back upstairs," Scar snarled.

"I'm lonely, Daddy." She pouted and batted her eyes.

"I'll be right up."

Satisfied, she obediently turned and went back upstairs. Arnold came from around the corner.

"Was that your daughter?" he asked Scar.

"What?"

"Was that your daughter?" Arnold repeated.

"No. She ain't my daughter." Scar looked at Arnold like he was stupid.

"Oh. I heard her call you Daddy. I just assumed."

"She a friend."

"Well, invite her tonight. The more the merrier." Arnold smiled.

Scar had no idea what to make of this crazy white dude. Was he for real? Were people in the country all this friendly, or was this dude playing an angle?

"Well, I'm off. The vegetables need tending. Got some real beauties to sell tomorrow at the farmers' market." Arnold walked toward the front door.

As he got about halfway to the door, he stopped and turned to Scar. "By the way, you might not want to leave so much cash laying around your house."

"What you say?" Scar was instantly on guard.

"I happened to see the money on your kitchen table. You should put that into a bank. I'll talk to my brother

Erik. He's a manager at the savings bank in town. He's a good guy. He'll set you up."

"I don't think so." Scar reached behind him for his gun.

Just as Scar put his hand on the handle of the gun, Flex came barreling through the front door.

"Yo, Scar!" Flex yelled out, thinking that Scar would be in a distant part of the house. He stopped dead in his tracks when he saw Scar and Arnold standing directly in front of him.

"Oh shit. I thought you'd be upstairs." Flex was holding a brick of cocaine.

Arnold saw the cocaine in his hand and started sweating. He realized at that moment that he was in trouble. The piles of cash, the cocaine . . . *These men are drug dealers!*

Scar pulled out his gun and smacked Arnold in the head, knocking him out cold.

"The fuck you doing back?" Scar yelled at Flex.

"I forgot I had this brick in the trunk. I didn't want to be driving around all day with this shit. You know people around here be gettin' pulled over for driving while black," Flex said.

"Goddamn. Now what we do with this nosey mu'fucka?"

"We got to dispose of him," Flex said matter-of-factly.

"Shit. Help me tie him up." Scar shook his head slowly.

Flex went out to his car and got some rope from the trunk. They proceeded to gag and tie Arnold up, and then they put him in the basement.

"Take them kids to do their shit then come back here. We take care of this snooping nigga later tonight."

Flex went out the front door, and Scar went upstairs to pound some pussy, while Arnold lay in the basement unconscious.

Chapter 7

My Own Private Crack Den

The cocaine had run out, and former mayor Mathias Steele was fiending for another bump. He had spent the last two days snorting coke, watching television, and pacing around his house. He had wanted to hatch a plan to exact revenge on Scar, the governor, and anyone else he felt had wronged him, but this didn't happen. His mind was scattered and racing in a coke-fueled frenzy. He couldn't keep focused on one thought long enough to follow it through. Whenever he would begin thinking about a plan, he would soon find his thoughts drifting back to cocaine.

Mathias had given up any hope of ever working in politics again. No one was taking his phone calls. He was an outsider now. All of his old government friends were ignoring him. He had lost his identity, his personality; he had lost the career he had worked so hard to build and wanted for so long. The only thing he wanted now was for the people responsible for his downfall to hurt as much as he did. Before he was going to make that happen, though, he needed more cocaine.

He wiped his index finger across the glass top of his coffee table, where he had been cutting his coke. Mathias was in luck. There was residue left on the table, and he swiftly rubbed it on his gums. With a renewed sense of energy, he put the gun in his coat pocket and stepped out the door. Mathias squinted and shielded his face as the bright sunlight hit his eyes like a lightning bolt.

"Damn." He went back inside for his sunglasses.

With his eyes now protected, he was able to comfortably function outside. He rushed to his car and drove the Cadillac to his new favorite spot, the dope house where he was becoming a regular. On the ride over, he couldn't decide on the music he was in the mood for, and switched between radio stations at hyper speed. He stopped on a news station that was replaying a speech by Governor Tillingham on the state of the city. Mathias couldn't concentrate because he was so angry hearing the governor's voice. He heard bits and pieces of the speech as he weaved in and out of traffic.

"Corrupt former mayor . . . asleep at the wheel . . . useless police force . . ." were a few of the quotes he heard that sent him into a simmering rage.

He pulled up in front of the house and scanned the area to make sure no one was watching him or had followed him. The cocaine was making him extra paranoid. No one had any reason to be following him. No one even cared about him anymore.

Satisfied that he wasn't being followed, he made his way to the house. He was getting anxious knowing that just beyond the door, he was going to get his hands on some coke. For Mathias, it couldn't happen fast enough.

He gave three quick knocks on the door. His palms were sweating. He wiped them on his pants. The door opened slightly, and he heard a man's voice.

"What you need?"

"An eight ball." Mathias wiped his forehead with his palm.

The door opened to allow Mathias entry into the dark house. There were three men sitting around the living room in a haze of marijuana smoke. They were all staring at Mathias as he walked in. Mathias looked out of place next to the three men, all wearing the typical urban out-fit—fitted baseball hat, oversized T-shirt, jeans hanging low on their hips, and brand new Nikes. Mathias, on the other hand, was wearing a blazer, a button-down shirt, slacks, and loafers. He might not be a politician anymore, but he still dressed the part.

"Gentlemen." Mathias nodded to the men. They said nothing.

"You need a ball?" asked the man who had let Mathias in.

Mathias jumped as the man spoke. He was definitely on edge and had forgotten the other man was in the room when he saw the three others.

"Yes." Mathias cleared his throat and swallowed.

The man went into another room and came back holding an eight ball of cocaine. Mathias's eyes widened when he saw it. He pulled out his cash and exchanged it for the coke.

"Look, do you mind if I try it out before I leave?" Mathias asked.

"Feel free, my nigga."

"Thank you. I didn't get your name."

"It's Best, 'cause I got the best shit in town." He laughed.

"Thank you, Best." Mathias sat on the sofa, stuck his car key into the bag, scooped out a mini pile of coke, and snorted it.

"Ah, that's nice." Mathias fell back into the sofa with a smile on his face.

"Told you I got the best shit."

"Yes, you do."

The three other men had turned their attention to the NBA game on the television.

"Hey, Best, let me ask you something." Mathias snorted another bump.

"What's good?"

"If I'm looking for Scar Johnson, do you know where I could find him?" He scooped another bump and snorted it.

"Nah, dude. He ain't been nowhere to be seen." Best lit up a blunt, feeling relaxed. With the way this dude was snorting coke, there was no way he was a cop. "I might know somebody who know where he is, though." He exhaled a big cloud of smoke.

"Oh yeah? Who?" The excitement in Mathias's voice was obvious.

"How much it worth to you?"

"That depends." Mathias was sensing he was about to get into a negotiation. This excited him. Besides all of the power, negotiating was his favorite part of being mayor. And he was good at it.

"Depends on what?" Best took a drag of the blunt.

"How close is this person to Scar?"

"Only like his right hand man."

"Well then, that could be worth something. If it was true." Mathias was grinding his jaw he was getting so high.

"Oh, it's true, my nigga. Belie'dat."

"I'll tell you what. I'll give you a thousand dollars if you tell me who it is."

"Bet. Let me see the money."

Mathias chuckled. "Hold on, young buck. I'll give you half now, and if you introduce me to him, I'll give you the other half." Mathias pulled out five hundred dollars from his pocket.

"A'ight." Best grabbed the money. "Dude's name is Flex. He come by to collect his cash, but it always be at different times. Never the same day or time, so I can't tell you when to come back."

"What does he look like?"

"He mad diesel. He always working out at the gym. He a young cat, too. Most times he wearin' a Ravens cap on his head."

"Well, you let me know when he comes around and I'll give you the other half." Mathias got up to leave and handed Best a slip of paper with his number written on it.

When Mathias got to his car, he didn't start it. He sat in the passenger's seat, going over the information he had just received. It wasn't much, but it was enough to probably be able to identify Flex when he came by to collect. Mathias planned to stay in his car and stake out the house until Flex showed, then follow him to Scar.

He took out his coke, looked around, and then his paranoia kicked in again. He felt too exposed, sitting there in his car. He started to get uncomfortable and started fidgeting. He did a bump and quickly put the coke away. This plan wasn't going to work.

Mathias got out of the car and went back up to the house. Same as before, he gave three quick knocks on the door.

"You forget somethin', nigga?" Best asked.

"I'll give you a thousand dollars right now if you let me stay here and wait for Flex."

"I don't know, nigga. You lookin' like five-o might scare my customers."

Mathias showed Best the cash.

"A'ight. But you gotta stay in the back room the whole time. I don't want to see your tight ass in the front room at all."

"Just keep me supplied with coke and I'll stay in whatever room you like." Mathias clenched his jaw.

Best opened the door, took the money, and showed Mathias to his room. There was a small bed, a television, and a nightstand in the room.

The drugs were obviously affecting Mathias's ability to negotiate, but he didn't care. He talked himself into thinking he'd won the negotiation. As long as he was high, Mathias felt like a winner.

"Comfy," Mathias said sarcastically. He sat down on the bed, placed his coke on the nightstand, and prepared to wait for his meeting with Flex.

Chapter 8

Chance Meeting

Tiphani slowly slid the key card into the slot on the door. The lock disengaged, and she quietly opened the door to her hotel room. She tiptoed to the bathroom, gently closed the bathroom door behind her, and turned on the light. She looked at herself in the mirror, pleased that she had gotten in once again without waking Cecil. Visions of the sex session she'd just had with the front desk clerk, Evan, flashed in her mind as she splashed warm water on her face.

For the past three days, she had gone to the lobby in the middle of the night to pay for their room and get some dick from the young clerk. She told herself that she was fucking the clerk so they could keep their room without any hassle. That might have been part of it, but she was really enjoying teaching the young man how to satisfy her. It was like an artist with a block of clay. She could mold him into whatever she wanted. She was making him into her perfect fuck machine. When her revenge on everyone was complete, she planned on keeping her new little toy around. Yes, she would have other men, but Evan would always be her boy on the side—until she got bored or he got too old for her liking. Then she would drop his ass and tell him to kick rocks.

Tiphani took off the wig she was wearing to help mask her identity and placed it on the counter. She smoothed out her natural hair and smiled at her reflection in the mirror. She was pleased with herself. She had found a man to help her exact revenge on her enemies, and as an extra bonus, she could fuck the hotel desk clerk whenever she wanted.

Standing there staring at her face in the mirror, Tiphani thought about her children. She hadn't thought of them in a while. As she was inspecting her features, she thought about her daughter, Talisa, and how much the little girl was starting to resemble her. She wondered where they were and if they were safe. Her post-sex euphoria was now replaced with sadness and guilt.

Ever since she fled to Florida, she hadn't thought too much about her children. The longer she was separated from them, the less she thought of them. She was actually enjoying the fact that she didn't have to worry about them and take care of them. This realization caused Tiphani to feel a huge sense of guilt. She was torn between wanting to be a good mother and wanting to make herself happy. If she was being truthful to herself, she was happier when they weren't around. When she pictured her future, the kids were never part of her visions. Tiphani was confused about her feelings. She didn't want to abandon her kids, but she felt happier alone.

"They would be better off without me," she said to her reflection. "I need to make sure they're safe, and then I can disappear. It's better for them." Her eyes started to tear up.

Cecil opened the bathroom door and startled Tiphani. She flinched and grabbed at her heart when the door opened.

"Who you talkin' to, baby?" Cecil asked.

"No one. Myself." Tiphani splashed water on her face again, trying to hide her annoyance that Cecil had interrupted her time in the bathroom.

"You ain't goin' crazy, are you?" Cecil smiled at his attempted joke.

Tiphani rolled her eyes as she wiped her face with a washcloth.

"You look good, ma." Cecil bit his bottom lip.

"Ugh. Get outta here with that tired-ass, corny line." Tiphani sat down to pee, not caring that he was in the room. "And why you bite your bottom lip? That shit is so played and not sexy." She wasn't trying to hide her annoyance anymore.

Cecil got angry at Tiphani's salty attitude. He knew that she had just sneaked into the hotel room and he was trying to look past it. In fact, he knew she had been doing it for the past three days. He had a mind to slap some sense into this bitch for her disrespect, but he restrained himself. He was well aware that Tiphani had offshore bank accounts with stacks of money, and he wanted a piece of it. He was going to play it right with her and get his share when the time was right. So, for now, he would have to play it cool, even though he was starting to become leery of her.

"Why you up so early?" he asked.

"I had to pee." With a look of *What are you, stupid?* on her face, she pointed to herself sitting on the toilet.

Her lie angered Cecil. He knew damn well that she had been out, and he was doing everything in his power to remain calm, but he was unsuccessful.

"I heard you sneak in a few minutes ago." He looked straight into her eyes, challenging her to answer.

For a second, Tiphani was caught off guard, but she quickly recovered. Without missing a beat, she answered. "Oh, I went downstairs to pay our bill. Evan's being cool and taking care of it so no one asks questions. I just need to make sure I keep paying."

"Really? Evan's being cool." He mimicked her words.

"Yes, really."

"It takes two hours to pay a hotel bill? You think I'm stupid? Are you fuckin' him?" Cecil couldn't hide his anger or his jealousy.

Tiphani laughed, not because she thought it was funny, but because of nerves. She was stalling to think of an answer.

"I'm not fucking him. We talk. He wants to go to law school and has lots of questions for me. Evan's a sweet kid."

"For the last three days he's been asking you about law school?"

Tiphani was in a groove. There wasn't a question Cecil could ask that would rattle her. "No. We talk about other stuff. I'm tryin' to stay on his good side and not cause any suspicion. I'm not tryin' to get caught."

Cecil didn't have anything to say to that. He looked at Tiphani and tried to read her face, to see if there were any signs of her lying. He never could read her very well, and he'd definitely never really trusted her.

Cecil had been suspicious of Tiphani ever since they left Florida. He'd come back from his first trip to Baltimore only to find her packing up all her shit. He'd just committed murder for her, and it looked like she was ready to leave him high and dry. Being a sucker for her sex skills, he'd ended up believing the story she told. She said she'd been cleaning the house of both of their fingerprints before they jetted from Florida. The more time they spent together, though, the more he realized he was probably being played for a fool. However, he'd come too far to get rid of her just yet. He deserved to get paid for the work he'd already put in, and the only way he could do that would be to get access to her offshore money. He would just have to keep on doing what he was doing and keep one eye on Tiphani at all times.

Tiphani felt uneasy as Cecil examined her. To break his thought process, Tiphani used the one weapon she always used with men. The one thing that she knew men were weakest for.

"Baby, you know you the only one I want to fuck. I can't get enough of your dick." This wasn't totally untruthful. She couldn't get enough of Cecil's dick, but she also couldn't get enough of most men's dicks. She was insatiable when it came to sex.

Tiphani got on her knees in front of Cecil and slowly pulled down his sweats. Cecil's manhood instantly sprang to attention. "Mmmmm." Tiphani moaned as she wrapped her hand around it.

Cecil grabbed the sides of Tiphani's head and she started to work on his erection. As usual, Cecil instantly forgot about his suspicions as he watched Tiphani do her thing.

Tiphani finished Cecil off with her head game, then climbed into bed and ordered room service. Cecil followed.

"We need to get our shit in gear. I'm done relaxin' in this room doin' nothin' but orderin' room service, watching movies, and fuckin'. It's time to hunt down our prey," Tiphani said.

"Just say the word. We eat, then we go." Cecil stretched out on the bed.

"No. I'm not going. You're going. I can't take no chances of being recognized in the streets." Tiphani needed some time away from Cecil.

"Just wear your wig like you been doin' when you go to the lobby."

"Fool, that's in the middle of the night and only one person is seeing me. Besides, one stupid wig ain't gonna fool no one in the streets."

Cecil sprang up from his prone position to a sitting position and got in Tiphani's face. "Bitch, don't you call me a fool. You will regret it."

Tiphani sucked her teeth. "Please. I dare you." She calmly got out of bed to create some distance between them. She was nervous, but she wasn't going to let Cecil see that.

"Don't test me." Cecil wanted to smack the shit out of her. He was getting sick of Tiphani's attitude, but the thought of all her money kept him in line once again.

Tiphani ignored him as she went and opened the curtains, letting in the morning sun. She looked out over the Inner Harbor.

Cecil went to the bathroom and started the shower. The hot water and steam calmed him down. He figured getting out and driving around would do him good, take his mind off his growing doubts about Tiphani's loyalty.

"I'll start the hunt." He walked out of the bathroom and started putting on his clothes.

Tiphani was eating an omelet off the room service tray. "Thanks, baby." She smiled. "I've written down addresses of spots that I could remember where Scar frequented. You could start there." Tiphani gestured to a piece of paper on the service tray.

Cecil picked up the paper along with a strip of bacon. He ate the bacon as he read over the list. "There's only three addresses on here."

"That's all I could remember."

"It should be enough to start with." Cecil shrugged his shoulders.

"Before you start, buy some throwaway phones so you can update me on what you find. I don't want you calling the hotel directly." She handed him a hundred dollar bill.

Cecil took the bill and one more piece of bacon and then walked out the door.

Cecil was cruising the streets of Baltimore, getting accustomed to the geography of the city. He had dropped the cell phone off with Tiphani and gone straight out on the hunt. It felt good to be out on his own. After being released from prison in Florida, he had spent almost all of his time with Tiphani. The only time he was away from her was when he came up to Baltimore by himself to murder the police chief and Dexter Coram.

He had stopped off at the first address on Tiphani's list, but the house was vacant. Now he was just driving and taking in the sights of Baltimore. He noticed a lot of hustlers on the streets. He thought about questioning them about their knowledge of Scar, but figured it would be a waste of his time. If they were on the streets, they probably never had any contact with the boss of the operation. Scar wouldn't waste his time with the street hustlers. Cecil thought his best bet was to find the mid-level hustler, one who had met Scar but didn't have total loyalty to him. Someone who thought he could run the operation better.

Cecil pulled up in front of the second house on the list. It was a small, red brick, one-story home. He checked his 9 mm to make sure it was ready for action. He wasn't going to trust these grimy-ass Baltimore cats for shit.

Cecil knocked on the door. He heard some rustling on the other side and felt as though someone was looking at him from somewhere. He looked around and saw a set of eyes peeking out from one of the windows. The eyes disappeared, and Cecil heard some muffled voices.

"Who is it?"

"I'm looking for someone."

"He ain't here."

"I'm also looking for something."

"We don't got it."

"You don't got any weed?"

"You a cop?"

"No, sir."

The door opened slowly and Cecil was allowed entry. "I like that, a nigga referrin' to me as 'sir.' That got a nice ring to it. Sir." The young dealer smiled and smoothed the air in front of his face with the palms of his hands like he was looking at his name on a billboard in Times Square.

Cecil took in his surroundings immediately—two stoned dudes on the couch and two dudes at the door standing on either side of him. He was outmanned for sure, but he figured the two on the couch would be easy to take out. Their reflexes would be slow due to how stoned they were. The two surrounding Cecil might be another story. As a soldier in the Army, Cecil had been highly trained in hand to hand combat, but these two looked like they could scrap. They could be a problem.

Let's try and get out of here with no problems, Cecil thought.

"What you say you need?" said the dealer who opened the door.

"I'm looking for the chronic. I heard you might be able to oblige a nigga."

"You heard right, partna." The dealer walked deeper into the room. "How much you need?"

"Let's start with a quarter, and if I like what I see, well, let's say I could be lookin' for some serious weight."

"You sure you ain't a cop? That shit sounds like a cop talkin'. Tryin' some entrapment bullshit on a nigga." He looked at Cecil out of the corner of his eye.

"I can assure you I am no cop. In fact, I'll buy a bag then sit down and smoke a blunt with y'all." Cecil thought this would be a good opportunity to put the men's fears to rest. With their defenses down, he figured he would have an easier time of getting information out of them. He also wanted to get a little buzz on.

"A'ight, a'ight. I like that. You a smooth cat." He went into the kitchen. When he came back, he tossed three different bags on the coffee table for Cecil to choose from. "They all weighed out. Take yo' pick."

Cecil inspected the bags and chose the greenest, hairiest-looking buds.

"Let's get high." Cecil opened the bag, sat on the couch, and rolled a blunt. He lit it, filling his lungs with smoke when he inhaled and relaxed into the couch.

"I didn't catch your name." He exhaled and passed the blunt to the young dealer.

"Best." He took the blunt and inhaled the thick, pungent smoke.

"Two-tone." Cecil told him his nickname. He reached for the blunt. "This some serious shit, my man. We ain't get shit this good in the joint, for sure." Cecil inhaled another lungful.

"Where was you locked up? Jessup? Hagerstown?"

"Nah. Nowhere 'round here. Down south. Florida. I'm up here on some business." Cecil passed the blunt.

"Word. You a businessman?" Best took a hit off the blunt.

"You could say that. I'm looking for a few dudes. One you may know. Scar Johnson."

Best choked on the smoke and coughed it out. "You the second nigga be comin' around here askin' about Scar. That nigga Scar got ghost a minute back. Nobody heard nothin' 'bout him."

Cecil cocked his head. "Who's the other dude lookin' for Scar?"

"Some rich-ass fiend. Tell you what. For the right price, I'll point you in that nigga's direction." Best arched his eyebrows.

Cecil needed to know who his competition was and why he was looking for Scar. He went into his pocket, pulled out cash, and counted out five hundred dollars he had stolen from Tiphani.

"This do you right?" He handed Best the cash.

"This'll do just fine." Best nodded his head and pointed to the back room. "Go talk to him. He be fiendin' out in the back."

"Anyone back there with him?"

"Nah. Just that sad-ass nigga by his self."

Cecil felt like he got played. He wanted to beat Best's ass, but he couldn't fault the dude for tryin' to make an extra buck. He probably would have done the same thing if he were in Best's position. So, instead of fighting to get his money back, he let it slide and made his way to the back room.

Before opening the door, he positioned his gun to easily draw and readied himself for a fight. He swung the door open and sprang into the room with the agility of a cat.

"What the fuck?" Mathias jumped away from the door and fumbled for his gun, dropping it to the ground.

Cecil saw the gun and immediately drew his and pointed it at Mathias. "Hold up, nigga," Cecil warned Mathias and picked up the stray gun.

Mathias was glistening from the sweat that covered his body. He was so wet he looked like he had just stepped out of the shower. He stood there shaking and jittery, with his hands help up in surrender. "Okay, okay. Take what you want."

"You lookin' for Scar?" Cecil grabbed Mathias's gun.

"Yes. Are you Flex?"

"Why you lookin' for him?"

"I need to speak with him. That's all." Mathias didn't know the mystery man pointing the gun, and he wasn't about to give up any information that wasn't needed.

"Why you waiting here? He supposed to be here?" Cecil asked.

"Best told me that Flex would know where Scar was."

"Who's Flex?"

"One of Scar's men. You're not Flex?"

"No. When is Flex supposed to be here?"

"I don't know. I was just going to wait for him." Mathias couldn't hold his arms up anymore. He relaxed them and they dropped to his sides.

"Put yo' hands back up! What's so important you need to speak to him?"

Mathias followed Cecil's orders, but this time, instead of raising them all the way up, he rested his hands on the top of his head. "You work for Scar?"

"If I worked for him, would I be looking for him?" Cecil looked at Mathias like he was an idiot.

"True." Mathias nodded in agreement. "Why are you looking for that snake?" He was thinking that since this guy was looking for Scar as well, perhaps they could work together.

"It sound like you ain't much of a fan of that nigga," Cecil said.

"I'm not. And by the looks of it, you aren't either." The energy in the room was beginning to relax. The conversation between the men was becoming more casual.

"That's right. What you after him for?"

"Can I lower my hands, please?" Mathias raised his eyebrows in a pleading way.

"If you try any stupid shit, I will put a bullet in yo' ass." Cecil kept his gun trained on Mathias.

Mathias slowly lowered his arms to his sides. "Ah, much more comfortable and civilized." He smiled and shook his arms to get the blood flowing back to them. "To answer your question, I'm looking for payback from Mr. Scar Johnson. That's why I am waiting."

"Payback for what?" Cecil asked.

"He ruined my career, and I plan on ruining him."

Cecil didn't say anything. He just stared at Mathias, trying to figure him out. He couldn't imagine what career this dude was talking about. He didn't look like a drug dealer, so Scar probably didn't move in on his turf. If anything, he looked like a sweaty-ass drug fiend.

The longer Cecil looked at him without saying anything, the more uncomfortable Mathias was getting. The more he looked at Mathias, the more Cecil felt like he knew this dude from somewhere.

"And you? You haven't told me why you want to see him." Mathias awkwardly broke the silence.

"Hold up. What career you in?" Cecil was trying to place where he recognized this dude from.

"Let's just say I was in a political office."

Cecil's eyes went wide. "Ooohhh shit! That's right. I knew it. You the grimey-ass mayor. I'm lookin' for you too. You look mad different, though. I didn't know you was some fiend. All sweaty and jumpy. No wonder you was corrupt. Your ass was needin' a fix." Cecil laughed.

Mathias ignored all of the insults being hurled at him. "Why are you looking for me?"

"I'm gonna kill you."

Mathias almost shit himself when he heard those words. His muscles locked up and he stood frozen. He wanted a line of coke.

"Wh—wh—why?" he stuttered.

"You see, like Scar ruined your career, you ruined my woman's career, and I promised to get revenge for her." Cecil cocked his gun.

"Wait, wait, wait, wait." Mathias put his hands up in front of his body like he was going to block the bullet. "I'm sure we can come to some agreement. Are you positive I'm the one who wronged your woman? I'll make it up to you—to her. Who is your woman?" Mathias was talking a mile a minute, saying anything that came to mind in order to stall for time.

Cecil cut him off. "Nigga, I know you the one I been lookin' for. You done fucked with my woman. She had a good ole job as a judge, and now she on the run."

"I promise, please, I'll do whatever it—Wait, did you say she was a judge?" Mathias stopped his babbling when Cecil's words actually registered.

"You have trouble hearing? Yeah, that's what I said, nigga."

Mathias started laughing uncontrollably, to the point of being almost psychotic. Cecil swore he could see Mathias's eyes glaze over with crazy. There was now a decision for Cecil to make: Put this crazy motherfucker down, or get some information out of him. He chose the latter.

Cecil side-kicked the laughing Mathias in his stomach. "Stop yo' fuckin' crazy-ass laughing."

Mathias doubled over from the blow, clutching his stomach at the point of impact. Although in pain, he continued to laugh. "Your 'woman' wouldn't happen to be Tiphani Fuller, would she?" Mathias stayed hunched over.

"Don't matter who my woman is. You fucked with her, and now you gon' pay."

"Go ahead, kill me. You're with that black widow; she's gonna eat you up and spit you out. Your fate will be worse than mine." Mathias cackled a demonic laugh.

"Don't tempt me, old man."

"Do you even know anything about her?" Mathias unfolded himself and looked directly into Cecil's mismatched eyes, one blue and one brown. It was Cecil's trademark, the reason his nickname was Two-Tone. "She's a manipulator, a user. She'll get what she needs from you and then leave your ass high and dry."

Mathias' tone made Cecil listen. It was the tone of someone who was speaking from experience, not someone who was begging for his life.

Cecil flashed back to the day he caught Tiphani trying to leave him in Florida. *I should have trusted my instincts then. I knew that bitch was grimy, but I let her talk me out of it,* he thought.

Mathias continued. "Do you even know what happened? I didn't run her off. She fucked with the wrong people and had to go into hiding so she didn't get killed."

"You were the one who tried to kill her," Cecil said, repeating part of the story Tiphani had told him.

Mathias let out one short burst of laughter. "Is that what she told you? I have known Tiphani a long time. She is a very driven woman and will do whatever it takes to get what she wants. She also has an insatiable appetite for sex, which helps her get what she wants. Men will do anything for her once they get a taste of her. Me included.

"I was fucking her for a while and she made me think I was special. Turns out she was making most of the men in City Hall feel special. Once I found that out I stopped it, but by then it was too late. She had gotten exactly what she wanted. She held it over my head, and in order to keep her from telling the world, I was forced to promote her and give her whatever she wanted."

"Sounds to me like you just got played. I won't let that shit happen to me." Cecil replied, although he wasn't feeling as confident as he sounded.

"You have already been played, my friend. You're out trying to clean up her mess. You know why she wants me dead? Because I was forced to have her arrested. You know why she wants Scar dead? So he doesn't kill her first.

"Look, Scar isn't a saint, and I want him dead as well, but that's for personal reasons. Tiphani is just mad because Scar played her. She started fucking him, and she fell in love. He used her and her judicial power to get himself acquitted. When things went bad for them, they went very bad, and now both of them are out for blood. But I can assure you that Tiphani Fuller is by no means an innocent victim.

"If you don't believe me, there are plenty of newspaper articles written about it. In fact, there's a video tape of Tiphani and Scar having sex. Feel free to look it all up."

Cecil was livid. This was exactly the opposite of what Tiphani had told him. She had painted herself as a victim, a sort of damsel in distress. Everything the mayor had just said made sirens go off in his head. His suspicions about Tiphani were stronger than ever. He was definitely going to do some research, but he was almost sure he was going to find out that Mathias was telling the truth.

This bitch thinks she can play me? She's sadly mistaken, Cecil thought.

"They say don't kill the messenger, but in this case, my brother, you about to die." Cecil smiled wickedly.

As his finger tightened around the trigger, the door to the room opened and hit him in the back, causing him to stumble forward and misfire. The bullet whizzed past Mathias's head and lodged into the wall behind him. In a split second, Mathias reacted and ran forward, knocking into Cecil and Best, who had entered the room. The impact of Mathias barreling into them sent all three tumbling to the floor.

The gun that Cecil had taken from Mathias landed right in front of Mathias's face. He quickly picked it up hopped to his feet and ran for the door. Cecil took aim and fired at Mathias. The bullet landed in the doorframe. Mathias made it through the door just in the nick of time.

Cecil jumped up in pursuit, knocking Best back to the ground as he frantically ran by him. Mathias haphazardly pointed his gun behind him and let off two shots as he ran out the front door. This stopped Cecil momentarily and gave Mathias a chance to separate from the melee. Lucky for Mathias, the three dudes who had been in the living room were nowhere in sight. They either hid when they heard gunshots, or had left before any of it started.

By the time Cecil made it to the front door, Mathias was nowhere in sight. There was no telling which way he had run.

Best came running up behind Cecil. "Yo, let him go. I don't need nothin' attractin' attention to my place."

"Fuck!" Cecil screamed as he scanned the empty street.

"Let's talk inside," Best said to Cecil.

"You right. Let's go inside."

When Best turned to enter the house, Cecil shot him point blank through the back of the head. No witnesses. That's how Cecil liked to keep it. The three dudes that saw him before would get theirs later.

Chapter 9

Common Ground

Sweat was dripping from Halleigh's forehead. She had been vigorously rubbing the toothbrush handle against the carpet for hours. She stopped and inspected her progress as she wiped the sweat away with her forearm. Unfortunately, the fibers on the carpet weren't do ing much to alter the shape of the handle. If anything, the back and forth motion of the rubbing had started to wear away the carpet and create a hole. The plastic on the toothbrush had barely been affected. Definitely not enough to satisfy Halleigh, especially with the amount of effort she had been exerting.

Halleigh sat and caught her breath for a moment as she tried to keep herself from getting discouraged. She kept her mind focused on her son, the main reason for her escape.

Sitting on the floor with her back against the wall, Halleigh's eyes randomly roamed the room. She was stuck. It was her prison. No way out except through the locked door. She had to start thinking like a prisoner. She had to fight for her life, and as she'd learned earlier, she wouldn't be able to overpower Derek; she just wasn't strong enough. The only weapon she had was a toothbrush, but at the rate that was going, it wouldn't be sharp enough to use for days, possibly weeks. Her situation was looking bleak.

The fluorescent light in the ceiling flickered and caught her attention. She was in a trance, staring at the tubed bulb when it hit her. She could use the light bulb as a weapon. She could swing it like a baseball bat at Derek. When it broke, she could use the broken glass to cut him and then flee. She contemplated breaking the bulb first and just using the glass, but was afraid Derek would hear it smash, thus defeating the "taken by surprise" tactic she was going for.

Halleigh reached up, stretching her arm as high as it would go, but was unable to reach the plastic covering. She thought for a moment then dragged the mattress and box spring across the carpet, placing it just underneath the light. Standing on her toes on top of the mattress she was able to extend and reach the cover. She removed the cover, exposing the fluorescent light. The bulb was too warm to touch, and she quickly pulled her hands away. The switch for the light was on the other side of the door. Even if she were able to turn it off, it would be a while before it would be cool enough to touch.

Halleigh heard movement upstairs. Derek was heading toward the stairs to the basement. She quickly took off her shirt, using it like an oven mitt as she turned the bulb and pulled it down. With the bulb in hand, she jumped down from the mattress and ran to the door just as Derek was opening it.

She swung the long bulb like a baseball player swinging at a fastball. It connected with Derek's left arm and exploded with a loud *pop*. Derek instinctively tried to shield his face from the attack. Halleigh leaped at Derek, attempting to stab him with the broken piece of

glass left in her hand, but he was too quick. His train-
ing on the police force prepared him for such attacks,
and he easily blocked her advances.

In one fluid move, Derek knocked the weapon out of
Halleigh's hand, spun her around, and forced her onto
the bed face down. Halleigh struggled to break away
from Derek, but he had her hands firmly secured behind her and his weight was too heavy for her to move.

"Calm the fuck down!" Derek commanded as Halleigh
continued her fight. She was like a wild dog that wasn't
about to be tamed—teeth bared, foaming at the mouth
and growling.

Derek had enough. He cocked his fist and punched her
in the back of the head. The force of the blow knocked her
out instantly.

Halleigh was disoriented as she slowly opened her
eyes. It took her a moment to figure out where she was
and remember how she had gotten there. She replayed
the attack on Derek in her mind. The last thing she
remembered was lying face down on the bed, hands
behind her, with Derek on top. She was still face down,
but when she tried to touch the pain stemming from the
back of her head, she was unable to move her hands.

Shit. I'm handcuffed. Halleigh unsuccessfully tried
to free her hands from behind her back.

"Welcome back." Derek was cleaning up the broken
glass strewn about the basement.

"Let me go." Halleigh squirmed on the bed, trying to
flip herself over.

"That ain't happenin'. Just relax."

"Fuck you."

"Listen, bitch. I could do some serious damage to you, to the point of killing your ass. So, if I was you, I'd shut the fuck up and just chill." He roughly flipped Halleigh onto her back and straddled her.

Halleigh looked into Derek's eyes with hate.

"Now look at this. I'm on top of a fine piece of ass and she don't have a shirt on." Derek traced a finger around Halleigh's upper body.

Halleigh remained silent. She clenched her jaw and braced herself for whatever was to come. From her days as a prostitute, she was able to mentally separate herself from a situation. She would just let Derek do whatever he wanted to do.

"What's the matter? You got nothing to say? You've been naughty and need to be taught a lesson, but if you're a good girl, maybe I'll let you go." Derek rubbed Halleigh's breasts over her bra. Halleigh still said nothing. Derek could see that she had checked out.

"Seriously, what the fuck is your problem? One minute you're attacking me every time I come down here, and now you're lyin' here like a rag doll. Bitch, I'm about to rape you. You should be fighting for your life."

Halleigh's eyes welled up and a single tear fell slowly past her temple into her hair.

"Goddamn, snap the fuck out of it. Speak." Derek slapped her across the face.

"What do you want me to say?" Halleigh's voice was just above a whisper. Tears were steadily streaming from her eyes now.

Derek didn't know what he wanted her to say. He was just pissed that she seemed disgusted by him. A small part of him wanted her to be attracted to him. He didn't want to rape her. Yeah, he wanted to fuck her, but he would never force himself on her. He was just playing mind games with her, showing her who was boss.

"Just stop being stupid and attacking me. I'll always win," Derek said.

"I'll never stop fighting for my son." Halleigh wouldn't look at Derek.

"You got kids?" Derek swung himself off of Halleigh and stood up.

"Just a son. He's the most important thing in my life. So, do what you want to me." Halleigh slowly turned her head to look directly at Derek. "But I will tell you this: I will never stop fighting for him. He needs his mama, and I will not let him down. Not like my mother did to me."

Derek couldn't bear to make eye contact with Halleigh. Her words hit him directly in the heart. He felt the same way about his children. He would do anything for them and would stop at nothing to protect them. He was feeling guilty because he was unable to come to their rescue. He was letting them down.

"What's his name?" he asked.

"Malek Jr. He's named after his father. I feel like I'm letting him down." The tears began again.

"I know what you mean."

"You have a son?" she asked.

"And a daughter. I would do anything for them. Including kidnapping. That's why you're here."

"Why me? I didn't do anything to your kids."

"You didn't, but Scar did. You're here so that your man will hurry the fuck up and help me find my kids."

"Day has nothing to do with that. Let me go. I'll find them for you. I'll help Day and we'll get them back." Halleigh's speech was rapid as she pleaded.

"I can't do that."

"Yes, you can. Our kids need us. I promise to find them. Just let me go. From a mother to a father, I promise. Please." Halleigh was sitting up. Hope was running through her body. She was going to appeal to the father in Derek. This was her chance.

"No!" Derek yelled.

"Please." There was desperation in her voice.

There was a long silence. Neither one said anything as they thought about their children, each feeling helpless. Each was determined to be there for their children any way possible.

"I'm sorry." Halleigh decided to change tactics.

"Just stop trying to overpower me, all right?"

"I'm sorry your kids got kidnapped. I understand your hurt. I would do the same thing if I was you."

"Thanks."

"It kind of turns me on, seeing a man fight for his family, doing whatever he has to to protect them. So many punks out there that wouldn't do anything. Takes a real man." She gave him a seductive look.

"The fuck you doing?" Derek asked.

"Nothin'. I'm just tellin' you like it is. It's makin' me a little horny."

"Stop the bullshit."

"Seriously, Daddy, take these cuffs off and I'll make all the hurt go away. I want you to take your anger out on my pussy."

"Yeah? You want Daddy to fill you up?"

Derek approached Halleigh slowly. Suddenly, she couldn't believe she hadn't played the sex card right from the beginning. Men were so stupid, always thinking with their dicks.

"Yeah, Daddy. Fill me up," she said, mentally preparing herself to pounce as soon as Derek uncuffed her.

Derek was standing right in front of Halleigh with a big grin on his face. "You think I'm stupid?" He punched Halleigh in her face as hard as he could, knocking her out cold for the second time.

Chapter 10

Truth Kills

Cecil exited the library on the warpath. He had gone on the library computers and read article after article about Tiphani and her affair with Scar. There was even a clip of the press conference the mayor had given where they played a blurred-out version of the video of Scar and Tiphani fucking. If there was one thing that Cecil couldn't stand, it was being manipulated. He figured himself to be pretty straightforward and he expected the same from others; so when someone was untruthful and trying to manipulate him, he took it personally. He felt it was his duty to teach the untrustworthy person a lesson, and that was what he was about to do to Tiphani. He would teach her not to fuck with people's emotions.

Driving back to the hotel, Cecil had a death grip on the steering wheel. His body was tense with anger as he thought about Tiphani. He was running through ways in his head to torture her, make her regret ever trying to play him. He would bring her to the brink of death, make her think he was going to kill her, and then back off at the last second as she begged for her life. Cecil still wanted her money, and killing her would lose him access to all of her offshore bank accounts. He might be angry and want revenge, but he wasn't stupid when it came to money. He knew where to get it, and he wasn't about to cut off his supply line.

By the time Cecil made it back to the hotel and parked the car, his emotions were a mixture of anger and excitement. He was looking forward to the torture and beating he was about to inflict on Tiphani. Torture may be against the law, but that didn't stop the military from teaching Cecil the intricacies of torturing information out of the enemy. There was a fine line between torture and interrogation, and Cecil was one of the best at walking that line. He was now looking forward to stepping over the line into torture territory. He always found it fun trying to find exactly the right technique that would put the enemy over the edge and make them spill all their secrets. Watching the enemy squeal in pain always brought a smile to his face.

Cecil walked through the lobby with focus and determination. He made a direct line to the elevators and pushed the button for his floor. His mind was occupied with torture techniques. He was running through the file cabinet of techniques in his head, contemplating which one to start with. Start slow and build to the climax was always Cecil's way.

The elevator doors opened. Cecil, still focused, walked out, turned right and headed down the hallway. He was on autopilot right now, his mind filled with visions of things to come.

He slid the key card into the slot and pushed the door to open. His shoulder met the door with a thud. The door didn't budge. He tried the card a second time. Again, the door didn't move. The third attempt yielded the same results. This time Cecil noticed that the red light came on, indicating the door was locked. He pounded on the door.

"Tiphani. Open the door." He waited for a response. Nothing. He pounded again. He listened for any movement on the other side of the door, but only heard silence. He stood there taking deep breaths, trying to calm himself.

Where is this bitch? He looked around the hallway, trying to figure out his next move. Did he go to the lobby and wait for her? Did he go drive around Baltimore so no one would get a look at him in the lobby? Tiphani was sure to get a good beating over this.

Cecil stepped back from the door and contemplated either kicking it or tampering with the locking mechanism. As he stared at it, he finally realized he was standing in front of the wrong door. He was standing in front of 1504; they were staying one floor up in 1604. Cecil hadn't been paying attention when the elevator doors opened. He had been in his own world and automatically stepped off, assuming it was his floor. Angered at his mistake, he kicked the door.

He started back down the hall, and as he was about to turn the corner, he heard the bell announcing the arrival of the elevator. Instead of running to catch the door, he slowed his pace when he heard a familiar female laugh. It sounded like Tiphani's laugh, and she was getting off the elevator. This confused Cecil. Did she make the same mistake as he did and get off on the wrong floor?

Cecil stopped in his tracks and waited to catch her off guard as she came around the corner. Standing there, Cecil heard a male voice as well.

Who the hell is that? Instead of the voices coming in his direction, they trailed off toward the other side of the hotel. He swiftly and quietly followed, rushing past the elevators and peeking his head around the other corner. He saw a man and a woman, their arms and legs intertwined, tripping over each other as they kissed and laughed their way down the hall. There they were all over each other.

It took all of Cecil's discipline not attack them. Tiphani and the front desk clerk were obviously about to go fuck. With his head just poking from around the corner, he watched them pause in front of a door at the end of the hall. Evan used a key card and opened the door. He stepped aside, let Tiphani enter first, and smacked her on her ass as she strutted past him. This prompted a little squeal of delight from Tiphani.

Once the door was shut behind them, Cecil softly walked up to the door and listened. It was quiet at first. He could hear muffled voices, but couldn't make out what they were saying. After a minute or two, Cecil heard Tiphani's familiar moans. Cecil imagined Evan's face between her legs. It took all of his strength not to pound on the door. His entire body was tense with rage. His suspicions had been right: Tiphani was fucking the young hotel worker.

If she thought she could lie to him and play him, she was wrong. All of the information he had learned recently about Tiphani—and now to catch her out in a blatant lie and fucking another dude—had Cecil about to blow a gasket. He had had enough. He started to walk away, but not before hearing the sound of flesh slapping against flesh and the loud screams of ecstasy from Tiphani.

Cecil violently poked the elevator button with as much force as he could muster. He needed to take his aggression out on something or someone, and the button was the first thing in his way. The doors opened to an empty elevator car, and Cecil pushed 16 on the panel with the same intensity as before.

With the focus of a surgeon, Cecil entered his room, went directly to the closet, and pulled out his duffel bag. Almost robotic in his demeanor and actions, he placed the duffel on the bed and checked the contents. Satisfied, he slung the duffel over his shoulder and left the room.

He exited the elevator in the lobby and focused his sights on the exit. He kept his eyes fixed on the front doors and made a direct line to them. Nothing was going to distract Cecil from his mission. He walked through the front doors and straight to the car.

Forty-five minutes later, Cecil was back in the hotel room. Tiphani was sprawled out on the bed. She was propped up against the headboard, watching the television.

"Hey, baby." He went directly into the bathroom.

"I missed you," Tiphani called out.

"I bet you did," he replied.

Cecil came out of the bathroom holding his duffel bag.

"I don't remember you leaving with your duffel," Tiphani said.

"I didn't. I came back to get it. You weren't here." Cecil turned off the television. "Where were you?"

Tiphani started rummaging through the minibar. "I needed to get out. I walked down to the water. You needed your bag. That must mean you found something."

Cecil couldn't believe how easy it was for Tiphani to lie. He wondered if she had thought about her alibi beforehand, or if she just came up with it. "I didn't find anything. No one knows shit. Why didn't you wear your wig if you were going outside?" he asked.

Tiphani touched her hair. "Oh. You're right. I forgot to put it on. I hope no one recognized me." She gave a quick, nervous laugh.

Cecil was in awe at how easily her lies came to her. She wasn't about to get tripped up by his questioning. "Yeah, I hope no one recognized you."

"When are you going back out to look for those evil motherfuckers?" She poured herself a glass of wine from the minibar.

"I'm not. Like I said, no one knows anything. The trail is cold." Cecil turned on the television again.

"What?" She turned to him.

"Did I stutter? I'm not going back out there."

"I thought you wanted to help. These men ruined me. They deserve to pay for that." Her eyes started to well with tears.

Cecil ignored her fake-ass tears. He knew she was making herself tear up for effect. "Speaking of paying, if you want any of these grimy-ass B-More cats to talk, you gonna have to pay up."

"Is that what this is about? You want money?"

"The money ain't just for me. Hustlers wanna see cash before they're gonna talk. I'm sure they know where Scar is. They're just not speakin' for free. Besides, I already took care and murked two of your problems, so a little paper my way wouldn't hurt."

"I thought you loved me. This was just about money?" Tiphani downed the glass of wine in one gulp. "You know I love you." She crawled onto the bed and pulled Cecil down on top of her. She was going to use the one thing in her arsenal that she always used. She was going to let her pussy do the convincing.

Tiphani ripped Cecil's shirt off of him and shoved her hand straight down his pants. Despite knowing that Tiphani was a liar and a cheater, he still wanted to fuck her. Cecil used all of his aggression to fuck her as hard as he could.

After an aggressive and at times violent bout of sex, they lay panting next to one another on the bed.

"I know you don't want to, but you're gonna have to pay. Those cats out there want money. We pay, we find Scar," Cecil said.

"You're right. I want that motherfucker dead." Blinded by her obsession for revenge against Scar, Tiphani easily agreed. She jumped out of bed and went to her purse. She took out a small notebook, flipped through the pages, and stopped when she found what she was looking for.

She picked up the phone, dialed a number, waited a few seconds, then punched in some numbers that she read off the page in the notebook. After a few more seconds she said, "Yes. I would like to transfer fifty thousand dollars. Yes. Same bank. Thank you." She hung up the phone and threw the notebook back into her purse.

"I'm taking a shower. You got my hair all knotted up." She looked at herself in the mirror. "Then I'm going out to pay whoever tells me where to find Scar."

"You sure I was the one that knotted your hair up? Some of that cash better be for me," Cecil said as she entered the bathroom.

As soon as Cecil heard the shower going, he jumped up from the bed and went to Tiphani's purse. This was a bit of good fortune for Cecil. She usually didn't let her purse out of her sight, even when she went to the bathroom.

Cecil quickly flipped through the notebook. He stopped and smiled when he found it. It was the numerical code to one of Tiphani's offshore accounts. He ripped the page out and stuffed it in his front pocket.

Meanwhile, Tiphani was in the shower trying to figure out what Cecil's last comment meant. Did Cecil know she had been fucking Evan? Tiphani convinced herself that there was no way he could have known that. She chalked it up to Cecil being a jerk.

Tiphani was mad that Cecil was not going to be helping her without getting paid, but she figured he was still her best bet. She calmed herself down and decided to pay Cecil. It would speed up the process of finding and killing Scar and Mathias. It was little to pay to get what she wanted. Plus, she figured she could get the money back from Cecil later on. She was confident that all she needed to do was fuck him and he would eventually do whatever she wanted.

After drying off, she came out to see Cecil still in the same position on the bed, watching television.

"I'll go get your money. You deserve it for being so strong and brave. I just need you around me, baby. I can't get enough of your fine self." She was obviously trying to butter him up.

"A'ight, baby. You know I don't like asking for money. Hurry back so I can put a hurting on that pussy." He leaned over and smacked her ass. She cooed and began to dress.

"Where are the keys, baby?" she asked.

Cecil reached in his pocket and threw the car key to Tiphani. She caught them in one hand and started for the door.

"Don't forget your wig. Can't have anyone recognize you and ruin it all." Cecil smiled.

"Oooh, you're right. I keep forgetting that shit." She lifted the wig off the dresser and adjusted it on her head. Satisfied with her appearance, she leaned in and gave Cecil a romantic kiss good-bye.

"Can't wait to taste you when I get back," she whispered in his ear.

"Hurry back," he replied.

Once she exited the room, Cecil turned off the television and then lay back with his hands behind his head, staring at the wall like he was thinking—or waiting. He took in the silence of the room. He was calm. Less than five minutes later, a huge explosion occurred outside. It shook the building. Cecil simply smiled, got off the bed, gathered his belongings, and calmly left the room.

When he got into the lobby, it was chaos. People were everywhere, running in all directions, screaming into their phones. Cecil walked coolly through the chaos and right out the front door. He glanced in the direction of the parking lot, the center of the chaos. He could a see large cloud of black smoke with a fire at its center. It was exactly what he'd expected to see, the aftermath of the type of car bomb he had planted in his car.

Tiphani had taken the car more willingly than he had expected. *I guess she won't be coming back anytime soon.* Cecil smiled to himself and kept walking into the heart of Baltimore.

Chapter 11

Good News, Change of Heart

Derek turned on the ignition and quickly reversed his car out of the driveway, causing the wheels to screech as the rubber fought for traction. The episode with Halleigh had Derek at his breaking point. He hoped she was dead. How dare she think she could play him? He was sick and tired of women thinking they could use sex to manipulate him. Tiphani had played him for years, and he would never allow that to happen again.

Good riddance, Halleigh. Hope you enjoy your grave, you conniving little bitch. You and Tiphani will make great friends in hell.

He was done waiting around for Day. He was going to take back control and take matters into his own hands. This cat and mouse game with Day needed to end. It was time for Derek to start his shock and awe campaign on the streets of Baltimore. His children had waited long enough; it was time for Daddy to rescue them.

Derek made the hour-long trip into Baltimore in a little over thirty-five minutes. He was passing every other car on the road, not caring if he was pulled over for speeding. He cruised into Baltimore and began his slow and methodical route around the city. He was going to hit all the hot corners and shake some things up.

At the first corner, a kid about thirteen years old saw Derek get out of his car and immediately ran the opposite direction.

Damn, I still have that cop look to me, Derek thought.

The next corner, he took a different approach. He stayed in the car and acted like he was copping. The young buck who obviously controlled the block sauntered over to the car.

"What's good?" the kid asked, leaning into the driver's side window.

"I'm looking for something," Derek answered.

"I got what you need."

"You know where Scar Johnson is?"

The kid backed up from the car. "Nigga! You think I'm a snitch? Kick rocks, mu'fucka." He walked back to his corner and stared at Derek with a scowl on his face.

Derek thought about getting out and kicking the kid's ass, but the three other kids standing next to him were probably strapped. He wisely chose to move on.

His approach to the next corner had to be different. He wasn't getting the results he wanted. He was impatient and didn't have time to draw this whole thing out.

Derek parked his car around the corner from his next destination. He walked around the block and made eye contact with the kid running the corner, mimicking what he had seen done many times while on a stakeout. The kid took the bait and approached Derek.

"You good?" the kid asked.

"I'm looking, but I think there's eyes on us. Follow me." Derek kept walking past the kid as he said this.

The kid looked around to see where they were being watched from then followed Derek around the corner and into a building. As soon as both of them were through the front door of the building, Derek spun around and slammed the kid against the wall.

"Yo, what the fuck!" The kid struggled to get away from Derek's grip.

"Shut your mouth." Derek put a gun to the kid's head.

A look of fear swept over the kid's face and he stopped struggling. "Take whatever you want. Money in my pocket, drugs is in my sock."

"I'm not robbin' you. I need some information from you," Derek said.

"I don't know shit," the kid pleaded.

"Where is Scar?"

"I told you I don't know. I ain't never seen that dude."

"Don't lie to me, motherfucker. Where is he hiding?" Derek pressed the gun into the kid's temple.

"I swear I ain't lyin'. His man Flex be handlin' the re-up."

"Motherfucker, tell me what I want to know." Derek shoved the gun in his mouth. "If you don't tell me in ten seconds, I will blow your head off. One . . ."

Tears fell from the kid's eyes as he struggled to break free. He was trying to scream, but the barrel of the gun was muffling the sound. Derek reached ten and removed the barrel of the gun from his mouth. The kid instantly started pleading.

"Please don't shoot. I swear I don't know nothin'. Please."

Derek looked into the kid's eyes to try to read his thoughts. He figured if the kid did know something, he wouldn't be punking out so easily. He was just some young teenage wannabe about to get swallowed up by the streets.

Derek put the gun to the kid's temple, stared into his eyes, and kneed him in the balls. The force of Derek's knee to his groin made the kid double over in pain. As soon as he leaned over, Derek slammed the butt end of the gun to the back of his head, opening a huge gash and knocking him to the ground.

Derek needed to come up with a different approach if he was going to get any answers. He got back into his car and slammed the door shut.

"Fuck!" he shouted. He sat there trying to calm himself. He needed his head clear so he could come up with a better plan. His mind wandered to Day and how useless he had been. If only Day had been able to get him some information faster, he wouldn't be out on the streets beating teenagers, and he would have his children.

It suddenly occurred to him that he knew where Day would probably be. He started the car and made his way to Halleigh's house. On his way there, he thought back to the last time he was at the house and how he had surprised Halleigh then kidnapped her. He would stick to the same strategy with Day. He would hide in the woods and wait for his victim.

When he arrived, he was pleased to see Day's truck in the driveway. He considered taking him by surprise while he was inside, but decided to wait. If he went up to the front door as he had done with Halleigh, there were too many windows that Day could look out. He would have a better chance of sneaking up behind Day as he made his way to the truck. So Derek went to the woods, to the same spot where he had waited the first time. He had a clear view of the front door, so no one was coming in our leaving without Derek seeing it.

Derek started getting hungry and impatient after waiting in the woods for two hours. He was starting to question whether Day was even in the house. He made a deal with himself that he would give it another hour then come back the next day.

Twenty minutes into his last hour, Derek saw signs of life coming from the house. The garage door opened up and Day out walked. Derek perked up and forgot about his hunger. He readied his gun and moved into position for the ambush.

Day stepped back into the garage, which gave Derek the opportunity to move even closer. He was crouching on the side of the house behind some bushes, ready to pounce as soon as Day came out again. His body was like a compressed spring ready to unleash.

Derek started to jump up when he saw movement, but immediately pulled back when he realized it wasn't Day. Instead, a little boy came bopping out. Derek retreated behind the bush.

"Yo, M..J. Wait up. Stay by the car," Day said from inside the garage. M.J. obeyed and waited by the passenger's side.

Derek watched as Day followed behind and pressed the button to close the garage door. Day then opened the back door of the truck and put M.J. into his car seat.

"When is Mommy coming home?" M.J. asked.

"Soon, little man. Soon. I promise," Day answered.

Derek saw sadness in M.J.'s face. He thought about his own kids and how they must be feeling. He felt guilty for keeping Halleigh separated from her son. Like Derek, she would do anything for her child.

He was conflicted now. On one hand, he could use Halleigh to get his own children back—although that approach was taking a lot longer than he had expected. On the other hand, he was keeping a mother from her child.

His guilt won out. He decided not to ambush Day. The kid was an innocent bystander; he didn't deserve to see any violence. Derek figured he would have just as much success hunting down Scar on his own.

He sneaked back to his car and drove back to his place in the country.

Derek was feeling helpless and useless as he thought of his children on the drive back. They were somewhere out in the world with that monster, Scar. He couldn't believe that his own flesh and blood had turned on him so severely. It was beyond Derek's comprehension to think that one brother could be so different from the other. His once-deep love for his brother had turned into an even deeper hate.

To try to think of something else and not end up killing himself for feeling so useless, he turned on the radio. Derek's thoughts were still swirling, and he was unable to fully focus on the radio. Soon, though, he found himself listening carefully when the DJ came on with a breaking news story.

Disgraced former judge Tiphani Fuller has been found dead. Police believe she was the target of a car bomb explosion in Baltimore this afternoon. Miss Fuller is the third government figure to be killed by a car bomb within the last few months. All government agencies have been put on high alert. . . .

Derek stopped listening after that. He was stunned. He didn't know how to feel about it. At one time, Tiphani had been the love of his life. He was going to grow old with her. They were going to watch their grandkids together. He had been devastated when he found out that she was fucking his brother. It was the start to this whole mess that he was now in.

He thought back to everything that had happened. This thing had gotten out of control. There had been too much death and mayhem, and now it needed to end. Derek was tired of fighting. He just wanted his children back and to keep them safe.

He chuckled to himself as he thought about it. He couldn't believe that he actually felt a little sad at hearing of Tiphani's death. His emotions were definitely mixed. Part of him was sad; the other thought she finally got what she deserved.

The only thing good that came from that woman was my children. Derek made a deal with himself: from that point on, he would never think about that woman ever again.

Getting back to the house, Derek started feeling more in control. He felt that he now had a better handle on how he would find his children. Instead of relying on Day, he would take matters into his own hands, and he would come up with a better plan than the ones he'd tried today. *If you want something done right, you have to do it yourself.*

He went directly to the basement. He wasn't sure if Halleigh was dead from his last punch, but in case she was alive, he wasn't taking any chances. He cautiously opened the door. History was not going to repeat itself and have Halleigh sneak-attack him again.

To his surprise, when he opened the door, he found Halleigh sitting on the bed, her hands still handcuffed behind her back. She looked like hell. Her face was swollen and bruised from the punches Derek had landed. Her hair was a mess, and her eyes were bloodshot.

"You got up." He entered.

"Fuck you," she spat.

"Thanks for not attacking me when I came in."

"I would have killed you if my hands weren't cuffed." Halleigh was done with etiquette. She had taken too much abuse, and her hopes for escape were fading.

Derek approached her carefully. He could see the wildness and uncertainty in her eyes.

"Back the fuck away from me," Halleigh warned.

"I'm not gonna touch you. Turn around. I'm taking your cuffs off." He held his hands up so she could see the key.

She contemplated whether to trust him. She was his prisoner; she figured she had no other choice. Reluctantly, she turned to give him a clear view and easier access to the cuffs.

She held her breath as he inserted the key and unlocked the cuffs. They easily slipped off her wrists and Derek threw them on the bed. Halleigh's breathing relaxed a bit as she rubbed the sore spots of her wrists where the cuffs had dug in.

She was a bit confused by Derek's attitude. His demeanor seemed different. He was less on edge and seemed almost at peace.

Derek started to walk back toward the door without saying a word. As soon as he turned his back, Halleigh reached under the mattress and pulled out the sharpened toothbrush. While Derek was away, she'd tried to sharpen the toothbrush on the metal of the handcuffs. Not being able to see what she was doing made it a difficult task, and she did the best she could. It was an uneven job, and she would have liked it to be sharper, but it would have to do.

She jumped up and lunged at Derek. With all of her strength, she tried to plunge the toothbrush into his neck. At the last second, he moved out of the way, and she jammed it into his shoulder instead.

Derek screamed out in pain as he flipped her over his shoulder and onto the floor. Halleigh had the wind knocked out of her, and as she writhed in pain, Derek pounced on top of her.

They were in a familiar position, Derek on top of Halleigh, pinning her down. Halleigh looked into Derek's eyes and saw evil. He reached back and pulled the toothbrush out of his shoulder. Blood immediately came oozing out of the wound. He raised the tooth-brush over his head, and with all the rage and force in his body, he brought it down, directed at Halleigh's head.

Halleigh closed her eyes and braced herself for the certain death about to overtake her. She heard a loud thud in her ear. She waited to feel the pain of the tooth-brush entering her face, but she felt nothing. The only sound in the room was Derek's heavy breathing.

Halleigh opened her eyes and saw him still over her, wild-eyed and panting. He had slammed the tooth-brush into the floor right next to Halleigh's left ear. His hand was still wrapped around the handle, and the toothbrush was stuck into the carpet.

"Why the fuck you keep attacking me? I was going to let you free." He pulled the toothbrush out of the carpet and got off Halleigh.

She was speechless. She had been certain that she was about to die. Unsure of what was happening, she stayed on the ground. She didn't want to provoke Der-ek into another attack.

Halleigh watched as Derek walked to the door. He stood there and stared at Halleigh like he was waiting for her to do something. She didn't know what he ex-pected, so she stayed put.

"Go! Get the fuck out of here. You're free. This thing has gone on long enough. It's between Scar and me." He motioned for her to go through the door.

Halleigh slowly got up, unsure if Derek was telling the truth or fucking with her emotions. She hesitantly walked past Derek. Walking up the stairs, she was still nervous, half expecting some surprise attack at the top of the staircase. She got to the top and was relieved when nothing happened. Her body began to relax.

Derek kept his distance as he followed her up the stairs, so as not to spook her. She found her way to the front door of the house.

"Wait," Derek said.

She stopped, thinking that was the moment when he told her he was lying. She felt defeated.

"You need some clothes." He went to the bedroom and came back with a sweatshirt and sweatpants.

"Thank you." She took the clothes and put them on. They were too big for her small frame, but she tightened them as much as possible.

"Go back to your son and tell him you love him." Derek smiled weakly. Sadness swept over him.

"I will. You do the same." She walked out the door not having a clue how to get back to her house. She didn't care. She was seeing the sky for the first time in a long time. She was free.

Derek watched her run down the long driveway until she was around the bend and out of sight. He was feeling melancholic. There was a bad feeling in the pit of his stomach.

This is not going to end well, he thought as he went to tend to the wound in his shoulder.

Chapter 12

Stay Away From the House

Talisa and D.J. came barreling through the front door with toys filling their arms. They ran directly to the living room, dumped their toys on the floor, and energetically ripped into them. Flex followed, looking exhausted. The kids had him running all over the toy store. He was afraid of what Scar would do if anything happened to them, so he had been extra cautious, not letting them out of his sight.

"Ay yo, Scar," Flex called out.

Scar came lumbering down the stairs when he heard the ruckus the kids were causing.

"Look at my new dolls." Talisa presented them to Scar.

"That's nice." Scar brushed her off.

"Where is Charisma? She said she would play with me," Talisa asked.

"Charisma, get your ass down here!" Scar yelled up the stairs.

Charisma quickly came down like an obedient dog.

"I got new dolls. Look. You want to play?" Talisa asked Charisma.

"Play with the kids," Scar ordered.

"Sure, I'll play with you, honey." She pursed her lips at Scar and sat on the floor to play with the toys.

"Speak to me in the kitchen," Scar said to Flex.

They both moved to the kitchen and sat across from each other at the table. The pile of cash was between them, still covering the tabletop.

"What we gonna do about the white boy?" Scar asked.

"We got to get rid of his ass," Flex said matter-of-factly.

"Goddamn." Scar shook his head in disbelief. "Why this fool had to be so nosey? I came out here to lay low and not attract any problems. Then this mu'fucka come snoopin' around."

"Maybe that fool is dead already. I'll go look." Flex got up to go to the basement.

Arnold started writhing around the moment he saw Flex. He strained against the ropes tied around his wrists and ankles. The chair he was sitting in was bucking back and forth. He was unable to speak or scream because of the gag stuffed in his mouth.

"Calm down, nigga. Ain't no sense in you actin' all crazy. Your snooping ass ain't escapin'." Flex stood in front of Arnold and smiled. He enjoyed watching the struggle.

Flex slapped Arnold across the face, which stunned him and stopped his struggle instantly. Arnold just stared at Flex in shock. The slap knocked him back into reality. He realized it would be better to relax and cooperate than to fight.

He had no idea how long he had been down in the basement. If only he could speak to them, he could tell them he wouldn't tattle on them. He would tell them that it was their business, not his, and they could use drugs if they wanted. Arnold wanted to tell them that he had smoked a little marijuana when he was a teenager. He figured it would show them he understood and passed no judgment against them. He wanted to assure them that he would not turn them in. If only they would take the gag out of his mouth, he figured he could make things right and be back home.

The doorbell rang as the two men stared at each other.

"Keep quiet." Flex went upstairs to check things out. He stuck his head out the basement door. "Yo, Scar. Who the fuck is that?" he whispered.

Scar cautiously peeked through the window. Standing at the front door was a woman in overalls, her brown hair in a bun on top of her head and a worried look on her face.

"It's some white bitch," Scar whispered back.

She rang the bell again.

"Ignore her," Flex said.

"Nah. I'll get rid of her." Scar went to answer the door.

Flex retreated behind the basement door, but kept it opened just a crack, so he could hear what was being said.

"Can I help you?" Scar greeted the woman.

"Hello, I'm Betsy, your neighbor. Arnold is my husband." She smiled weakly.

"So what?" Scar answered rudely.

"Well, I came home this morning from the post office and Arnold wasn't there."

"What that got to do with me?" Scar was trying to be as rude as possible so she would get the hint and leave.

"I thought he might be out in the fields, but after a few hours I started to get worried. I went out there, but I couldn't find him. I called all of our friends, and no one has seen or heard from him."

"He probably ran out on y'all."

"No. His car is still in the garage, and I don't find you're comment funny. Have you seen him today?"

"He ain't been over here, if that's what you're askin'."

Betsy looked into Scar's eyes. She had a bad feeling about this man. It wasn't just the scar on his face that frightened Betsy; it was something behind his eyes. There was a danger lurking in this man. There was no reason for him to be so rude to her. She was worried about her husband and just wanted to find him. She wasn't expecting such attitude from her new neighbor, especially after her husband had gone out of his way to welcome him to the town.

Flex crept back down the stairs.

He pulled a gun on Arnold. "It's your bitch. She snoopin' around askin' questions about you."

Arnold began struggling wildly and trying to scream. He was hoping to make enough noise so Betsy could hear him.

"You best stop with that shit," Flex seethed through clenched teeth.

Arnold ignored his warning and continued trying to alert Betsy.

Flex cocked the gun and pointed it at Arnold's head. "I'm warning you, nigga. If you don't stop, I will go up there and murk your bitch."

Arnold stopped flailing and his scream turned to a whimper. Flex quietly sneaked back up the stairs. He peeked through the crack in the door. Scar was standing at the door, holding his gun behind his back. His finger was on the trigger, ready to shoot.

"I'm starting to get very worried. This isn't like him to disappear. Are you sure he hasn't been over here?"

"I told you I ain't seen him. How many times I have to say it?"

"I'm sorry to worry about my husband and think that you might be able to help," she said sarcastically. "You have made it very clear that I am bothering you. I know this is asking a lot from you, but if you see him, tell him to come home immediately." Betsy turned and went back toward her house. She was furious at Scar for his rudeness. Never had she ever experienced someone so cold. She sensed there was something going on at that house. She did not trust her new neighbor. Little did she know how close she had come to her husband—and to death.

Scar closed the door behind her. Arnold heard the door close and he started his screaming again.

"I told you to shut the fuck up!" Flex screamed down to Arnold.

Scar opened the basement door. "What the fuck you screamin' about?"

"This mu'fucka won't stop squirming and screaming like a bitch."

Scar was heated from the confrontation with Betsy. He didn't need no white bitch snooping around like her nosey-ass husband.

"Let's take care of this fool then take out his old lady. Get him ready to take outside," Scar said.

Arnold went crazy. His eyes were bloodshot and tears were streaming down his face. His throat was getting raw from his attempted screaming. The ropes were cutting into his wrists and ankles and causing them to bleed. Arnold didn't feel any pain at this moment. The only thing on his mind was getting free and saving his beloved wife.

Flex tried to subdue Arnold and release him from the chair. He attempted to untie Arnold's left hand and hold it still. As soon as his wrist was free, Arnold wrestled it away from Flex and removed the gag from his mouth.

"Please, please. This is a misunderstanding." He was holding off Flex and keeping the gag away from him. "I won't tell, I promise. I just wanted you to feel welcome."

Flex flipped the chair and Arnold onto his side. This temporarily halted Arnold's speech, but he quickly started up again.

"Let me go. I'm a simple farmer. I don't know anything. I'll leave you alone."

Flex wrestled the gag from Arnold. "Shut yo' mouth."

Before Flex could stuff the gag back in Arnold's mouth, Arnold screamed, "Help!" He screamed so loud that he strained his vocal cords, but to Arnold it felt like he had ripped them.

Scar ran up the stairs. "Yo, Charisma, take them kids upstairs," he yelled.

"Uncle Scar, we're not tired. We want to keep playing," Talisa called back from the living room.

"If you don't go upstairs, I will put a serious beating on your ass," he threatened.

The kids could hear a different tone in their uncle's voice. He meant what he was saying, and the kids obeyed at once. Charisma followed right behind, not wanting to get in the path of a raging Scar.

By the time Scar got back downstairs, Flex had Arnold restrained and lying on the ground. Fear was all over Arnold's face. He never thought he would be in a situation like this. He was a simple man who lived in the country because of the quiet life it afforded him.

He loved his wife and his life, and he never harmed anyone. Never would he have imagined dealing with monsters like Scar and Flex. Their evil was too much for Arnold to comprehend.

"Pick him up. Take him out back," Scar instructed.

Arnold fought back as best he could, but he was running out of strength. His muscles were feeling heavy and unresponsive. Flex tried picking him up, but Arnold wouldn't stay still and was making it too difficult. Flex punched Arnold several times in the face until Arnold was unconscious.

Scar and Flex picked him up and carried him deep into the woods behind the house. Along the way, Arnold had woken up, but he was still so dazed he wasn't able to do anything. He tried to pay attention to where he was and how long they had travelled, but it was useless. His brain was too hazy to figure anything out.

"A'ight." Scar stopped walking and let Arnold go. Flex did the same.

Arnold landed with a thud on a bed of pine needles. He looked up from the ground and could see that tall pine trees surrounded them. He knew exactly what part of the forest he was in. This was Arnold's favorite place to stroll by himself.

He watched as Scar and Flex hovered over him. They were discussing something, but he couldn't hear what they were saying. Everything was muffled, like he was wearing earplugs. He was having trouble focusing his eyes. It would all become blurry when someone moved. The punches to his face must have dislodged a nerve in his eyes.

Scar looked down at Arnold. "Damn, this sorry fool. You think he really was being nice?"

"I don't know. Either way he a dumb mu'fucka. He should have just kept to his self," Flex answered.

"You right. This shit is the real world. It ain't no TV show from the fifties. Not everybody be wanting their neighbors all up in they business." Scar looked down and studied Arnold's swollen and bruised face.

Arnold looked at Scar and pleaded with his eyes. His body ached and his head was throbbing. Scar's face was blank. Arnold could see that anything he did now to survive was useless. He didn't want the last thing he saw to be the face of a monster, so he moved his gaze to the trees. Arnold loved the land and always felt at peace surrounded by these trees. He was now looking to the trees for comfort in his final minutes.

"Wrong place at the wrong time," Scar said to Arnold.

Two shots rang out and echoed through the forest. Arnold lay motionless, with two bullet holes through his head. The blood poured out of the holes and seeped into the earth. Scar and Flex stood in silence as they examined the corpse. After a few moments, Flex broke the silence.

"Oh shit. You almost blew that mu'fucka's head clean off."

"Go get some shovels. We need to bury the body," Scar instructed.

"For real? Some bear will probably eat him if we just leave his ass."

"Just do what I say."

"A'ight," Flex begrudgingly agreed.

Flex left Scar there and started the trek back to the house. He didn't see the point in burying the body. It was just some stupid white boy who the animals would tear to shreds. No one would find him before he was ripped up and unidentifiable. Burying him was more work than they needed to be doing.

Flex was getting sick of having to take orders from Scar. There were a lot of things that Flex would do differently. To Flex, not only would they be different, but they would be better. Flex would ride with Scar for a little while longer, but it would soon be time to branch out on his own.

Before he could go out alone, he would need to figure out an escape plan. He still had loyalty to Scar and wanted to avoid the usual murdering of the king to take his throne. He wanted to find a way for both of them to split the kingdom evenly.

While Flex navigated his way out of the woods and contemplated his future, his phone started ringing.

"What's good?" he answered.

"What the fuck? I been calling your ass like crazy and your phone be off," said the young corner boy.

"Nah. I'm out in the middle of nowhere. Reception is shit. What's so urgent you keep calling?" Flex asked.

"This cat Day be around here asking about you. Say for me to give you his number if I see you. You want me to murk that dude?" The corner boy was hoping the answer would be yes. He saw this as an opportunity to gain some street cred. He would have done it already, but he wanted to make sure that was what Flex wanted. He saw Flex as his way to move up, and he would do anything Flex wanted.

"When was this?" Flex stopped walking.

"Yo, a few hours ago. I been trying you ever since. This ain't the first time this nigga be around here. First time, I ignored his ass and threw his number out. What you want me to do?"

"You keep his number this time?"

"I got it."

"Text me that shit. Sit tight and don't do nothin' right now."

"A'ight." The corner boy hung up.

Flex received the text as he was making his way back to Scar and the dead body. Scar was sitting next to Arnold on the ground, looking up at the sky when Flex came back.

"Where the fuckin' shovels?" Scar asked.

"Change of plans. Day surfaced, and he lookin' for us."

"What?" Scar stood up.

"Got a call from my boy. He gave me Day's number. Says Day been stopping by, asking questions. What you wanna do?"

"Call that disappearing mu'fucka," Scar said.

Flex dialed the number.

"Where the fuck you been, nigga?" Flex started right in when Day answered.

"Flex?"

"Who the fuck you think this is?"

"Yo, I'm glad I finally found you. Shit's been crazy," Day said.

"Like I asked, where the fuck you been?"

"I heard they raided Scar's place. I ain't know what was goin' on, so I went underground. Once I figured it was safe I came out, and I been looking for you ever since. You ain't easy to find. Niggas went deep into the shadows."

"I been right out in the open," Flex told him. "Fuck them pig mu'fuckas. They can't touch me."

"Where you at? I need to get some work in."

"Hold up, nigga. You disappear and you think you can just come back like that? I got to run it by Scar." Flex looked over to Scar. Scar nodded his head.

"Come on, man," Day asked. "My pockets be light since all this shit went south."

"It ain't go south for me. I don't let nothin' affect my paper," Flex bragged. "I'ma text you where to meet. You best be here pronto, nigga."

"Tell me where to go. I'm leaving now."

"And don't be thinkin' of comin' here with anyone other than your own self." Flex ended the call.

"What you think?" Scar asked Flex.

"You know I never trusted that nigga." Flex frowned.

"Let's see what he got to say for his self. We'll bury this fool later." Scar started back toward the house.

Betsy was standing at her kitchen sink washing dishes when she heard two loud blasts echo through the woods. Her nerves were on edge, and the sound startled her. The plate that was in her hand shattered when it hit the floor. With hands shaking, she made her way to the living room and picked up the phone. She dialed the phone and waited for an answer on the other end.

"Yes, this is Betsy over on Shunpike Road. Can I speak with Officer Maki, please?" She waited for the officer to transfer her call.

"Hello, Betsy," Officer Maki answered.

"Hello, Adam. I need your help. Arnold is missing, and I think my new neighbors have something to do with it."

"What do you mean?"

"Well, I haven't seen Arnold, so I went to our new neighbor, and he acted very strange. I didn't get a good feeling from him. There was an evil to him. I think I just heard two gunshots in the woods, and I'm terrified that it . . ." Her voice trailed off and her eyes filled with tears. She couldn't bear to bring herself to say the words she was thinking.

"Betsy, it's all right. I'm sure Arnold is fine," Officer Maki assured her. "He'll show up. But I'll go over and check things out. Can you give me a description of your neighbor?"

"Yes. He is a large black man, and he has this unsightly scar that disfigures his face." She sniffled and dabbed at the tears in her eyes.

"Betsy, did you say he has a scar on his face?" There was concern in his voice.

"Yes."

"Do not go near that house again. Do you hear me? Stay away from that man." Officer Maki's tone had changed from reassuring to alarmed in an instant. There had been a statewide bulletin sent out with Scar's picture on it. If Officer Adam Maki was right, the state's most wanted man was hiding out in his little town.

Chapter 13

Crack Effort

Mathias crept out from behind the dumpster after the anonymous car drove by. He put his gun back in his pocket and looked up and down the block before continuing on his way to the dope house. He had become increasingly more paranoid after his run-in with Cecil. Everything was starting to frighten him. He saw danger in every car that passed and every person who looked his way. It didn't help that he had graduated from snorting cocaine to smoking crack. He had convinced himself that it calmed his nerves, but it only made him jumpier and more agitated.

He hated to have to go outside. The only time he left his house was to buy more crack, which was becoming more and more frequent. He was dipping into his savings to feed his habit. He had all but given up on looking for new employment. All of his old allies were now enemies to him. No one would take his call. He had even applied to a local fast food restaurant, but they could see "crack fiend" all over his face and wouldn't even interview him.

Mathias's eyes darted from side to side as he scurried down the street. The quicker he got to the house, the sooner he could be back home safe and sound. He would have preferred to drive, but he had traded his car to his previous dealer for three months of free crack. Their deal ended almost immediately, when the dealer got pulled over, got into a shoot-out with the cops, and was killed.

He made it to the building and knocked. A set of eyes peeked through a slot in the door.

"What?" the person behind the door barked.

"I need weight," Mathias answered.

The door opened halfway, and Mathias slipped through. There was another man standing there, who led Mathias down a dark hallway to the back room. There sat a fat man behind a table. He was surrounded by another three dudes, all holding automatic weapons.

"Speak," the fat man said.

"I need four eights of rock." Mathias was on edge. The three men with the weapons were making him nervous.

The fat man pulled a shoebox out from under the table. He removed four eight balls of crack and placed them on the table.

"There you go, big man."

Mathias pulled out the money and laid it on the table. The fat man counted it.

"All good. Take yo' shit and get the fuck out."

Mathias obeyed. He quickly took the bags stuffed them in his pocket and hightailed it out of the house. Once outside, he rushed to find a place to take a hit. He was all worked up and needed a hit to make his mind right.

He found an alley and ducked in, then sat behind a dumpster and prepared the pipe. The first hit went into his lungs, and Mathias was flying high. He sat there with his eyes closed, enjoying the ride. Then he felt a kick to his ribs. He opened his eyes to see a skinny little teenager standing over him.

"Give me your shit, crackhead." The boy kicked Mathias again.

Mathias scrambled to get away from the boy. The boy kicked him again. Mathias was trapped between a wall and the dumpster. He had nowhere to run.

"I said give me yo' shit or I'll kill you." Another kick to the head.

Mathias got lightheaded. He fumbled in his pockets. The boy backed up, thinking Mathias was going to give him the crack. Instead of the crack, Mathias pulled out his gun and blindly shot at the boy. The shot hit the boy directly in the chest, bringing him crumbling to the ground.

Mathias jumped to his feet. His eyes were wide with fear and surprise. He had never shot anyone. He watched the blood drain out of the boy's chest, staining his white T-shirt red. The boy was making gurgling sounds as he struggled to breathe.

Out of panic, Mathias ran as fast and as far as he could go. When he could no longer run, he slowed to a walk but kept on moving. He needed to create as much distance between the shooting victim and himself.

Unable to go any farther, Mathias found some shelter in a small park near City Hall. He was panting and sweating. He found a corner of the park and sat under a tree that would do well to hide him from prying eyes while he smoked his rock. He wiped the sweat from his brow and packed his pipe.

The anticipation of the high made Mathias forget about the incident he had just run from. He torched the rock and inhaled deeply. The smoke penetrated his lungs, and the chemicals entered his blood stream and shot straight to his brain. He felt the rush of the crack surge through his body. He took another hit, then another.

Mathias couldn't stop himself. He kept hitting the pipe, smoking the rock, and then repacking for another round. He finally took a break, but only because he was jittery, uncomfortable, and mumbling to himself. He was sitting under the tree, scratching all of the itchiness throughout his body. He had burned through an eight ball in under an hour.

"Keep it moving, buddy." The policeman standing over Mathias startled him and made him jump. The former mayor hadn't tended to his hygiene in a while. His clothes were tattered, his skin was dirty, and his beard was overgrown. The officer, not really paying much attention, didn't recognize Mathias.

"What?"

"You gotta move. Can't stay here," the officer replied.

"This is a public park. I can sit wherever I want," Mathias countered.

"Not today you can't. Get up."

"I know the laws. You can't kick me out of here."

"Yes, I can and I am."

"Well, I'm staying, and there's nothing you can do."

"I'm warning you. If you don't stand up now and vacate the park, I will arrest you." The officer unlatched his handcuffs from his belt.

Mathias contemplated standing his ground and continuing to argue, but saw that he was pushing his luck. If he got arrested, he would be frisked, and then he'd be without his beloved crack. He definitely didn't want that to happen. Mathias begrudgingly obeyed the officer.

Before walking away, Mathias took note of the officer's name. "Bullshit beat cop. I'll get him fired when I'm back in power," he mumbled as he skulked away.

"What did you say?" the officer called to Mathias.

"Nothing," Mathias shot back and kept on moving.

Mathias was still mumbling to himself about his run-in with the officer as he walked into a crowd of reporters and citizens gathering in front of a podium at the entrance to the small park.

"What's this?" Mathias vigorously scratched his neck.

"The governor is going to give a speech." Disgusted by Mathias, the photographer eased away from him.

Mathias's body tensed up and his heart began to race. This was the reason he was being kicked out of the park.

It's not enough for him to ruin my career and force me out of office. Now he has to humiliate me by kicking me out of the park. Mathias was exaggerating everything in his mind. The governor had no idea Mathias was anywhere near the park. The copious amounts of crack were starting to affect Mathias's common sense.

The anger coursing through his body caused Mathias to become even more fidgety. He couldn't stand still. The man who had destroyed his life and backstabbed him was going to be in front of him at any moment. Should he leave, or should he stay? He couldn't decide what to do. This could be his chance to humiliate the governor in public and get his position back. But how could he do it? His mind was unclear and unfocused, which was making him more and more agitated.

Mathias looked up to see the governor's motorcade pull up across the street. A rush of excitement came from the crowd as the reporters saw the governor exiting his car. Before he knew it, Mathias was pulling out his gun and running across the street.

"You ruined my life, you backstabbing piece of shit."
Mathias started shooting with the precision of a blind
man. The bullets were flying in every direction.

Screaming and shouting could be heard as the crowd
scattered. Like a well-choreographed dance, police officers jumped on top of Governor Tillingham to shield
him; others covered members of his cabinet, and the
rest surged toward Mathias. Making it farther than one
would think, Mathias emptied his gun of bullets before
being violently tackled to the pavement.

"Drop the weapon!"

"Get the fuck off of me!" he shouted

"Stay down! Arms behind your back! Don't move!"
Officers were shouting at him from every direction.

"Leave me alone! I order you! Do you know who I
am? That man is a criminal." Mathias struggled against
the weight of three cops. They had pried the gun away
from him and cuffed his hands behind his back. They
were going out of their way to handle Mathias as
roughly as possible, pressing his face into the pavement as they frisked him.

"A fucking crazy crackhead." One of the officers
pulled out the crack from Mathias's pocket.

"That's not mine."

The cops jerked Mathias up and shoved him into a
black Suburban with the darkest tint on the windows.
They all piled in and sped off in a caravan of police cars
and SUVs, lights and sirens at full strength.

"Enjoy the view out the window now, crackhead. It
will be the last time you ever see the outside world.
Your life is over."

Chapter 14

Not So Welcome Back

Day pulled up in front of the house after the long drive into the country.

"You need to behave when we go inside," he said to M.J., who was quietly sitting in the back.

M.J. just nodded. He was becoming more emotionally cutoff the longer he was separated from Halleigh. His bright and cheery personality was becoming introverted. Day noticed it, but he couldn't do anything to prevent it. He was busy dealing with the stress of finding Derek's kids so he could reunite M.J. with his mother.

They were deep in the country. Crickets, owls, and peepers all sang their songs and came together in a symphony only heard at night in the country. Day took M.J. out of the backseat. They both stood next to the car surveying the house. Day was looking for any signs of an ambush. He knew that Flex had it out for him, and because of the tone of their phone call, Day had a feeling that Flex might act up. He saw nothing suspicious. M.J. sat in awe at the size of the house.

Day and M.J. guardedly walked hand in hand toward the front door. From the side of the house, Flex came sneaking up next to them. He pounced on Day and put him in a chokehold. Day managed to stay on his feet as he fought against the attack, but Flex had him beat.

"You finally come out of hiding, punk ass?"

"Yo, chill," Day said through choked breaths.

M.J. was paralyzed with fear. He stared at the clash with eyes wide open.

The struggle continued.

"Stop," M.J. said softly.

The two men kept scuffling.

"Stop," he said louder and hit Flex on his thigh.

The tiny tap on the leg caught Flex's attention. He spun to see what had hit him.

"What? You brought a kid to help you fight? Ha!" Flex chuckled as he released Day.

Day bent over and rubbed his neck, taking time to catch his breath.

"What's up, little man? What's your name?" Flex approached M.J.

"Leave . . . him . . . alone." Day's breathing was labored.

"What the hell you bringin' a kid for? Thought I told you to show up alone."

"I . . . had to."

"Get yo' ass inside," Flex barked.

Day entered the house with M.J, following. They stood just on the other side of the door and waited for Flex. Before Flex could dole out any more punishment or orders, Scar came from another room.

"Well, well, well. Look who came out of hiding." Scar carefully eyed Day as he walked up to the trio.

"Yeah, and he brought some protection along with him." Flex laughed at his own joke.

Day ignored Flex. "What's up, Scar? It's been a minute."

"You damn right it's been a minute. Who the hell is half pint over here?" He gestured to M.J. with a head nod.

"Yo, he my son. I had to bring him. It's a long story."

"I got loads of time, nigga. Enlighten me."

Day was caught off guard. He wasn't ready to have to explain who M.J. was and why he was there.

"Oh, ah, well, you see, okay, you want to know. . . ." Day had no idea what to say.

"Spit it out, nigga." Flex shoved Day in the shoulder.

Scar just stared blankly at Day. It made Day feel uncomfortable, like Scar could see right through him.

"Like I said, he's my son. My baby mama, me and her don't really have much communication. Well, I found out she got hooked on the pipe and my little man here was being neglected. So . . . you see, I found this out right around the time I was lookin' for a place for you. That's why I was a little off about securing that spot I was tellin' you about."

Scar just stared at him like he was waiting for him to continue. Day continued to make up a story.

"I had secured that spot for you, and I was heading to let you know. That's when I drove by your place and that shit was swarming with all sorts of FBI, DEA—"

Scar interrupted. "You don't gotta tell me who all was there. I know." He leaned against the wall and glared at Day. "I've heard enough of your babbling anyway. Now I'm gonna ask questions, and I want answers. First, where the fuck you been?"

"I went deep underground. Seeing all of that shit, my first thought was that you got picked up. I was plannin' on staying real low until I heard otherwise."

Flex and Scar exchanged a look.

"You heard otherwise? That's why you out looking for me?" Scar asked.

"I didn't hear nothin' about you."

"Where were you 'deep underground'?"

"I was at the place I had found for you," Day continued to lie.

"When I'm gonna see this place?"

"Whenever you want."

"How about right now?"

Day was about to lose it. If Scar took him up on his offer, he was fucked. It would be the end of Day if he couldn't take Scar to a house.

Day was scrambling his brain to come up with a plan to get out of this mess when M.J. took off running into the living room.

"M.J." Day called out.

M.J. ignored him and kept on heading to the next room. Day started to chase him, but Scar stopped him.

"Don't worry about that. We got business to attend to." Scar put a hand on Day's chest.

Day's knees got weak. "He shouldn't be runnin' around. I'll get 'im."

"He's fine. He probably saw toys in there. Let the big boys stay in here."

Hearing the word "toys," Day figured that Derek's kids were close by. He attempted to change the subject right away.

"Yo, you got any work for me? I need to get back on the grind."

"Don't get ahead of yaself. You don't just come waltzing yo' ass back in and expect to be welcomed with open arms. You still got some questions to answer."

"A'ight. Ask away." Day acted like he was standing strong, but inside he wasn't so confident.

"First off, why the fuck we ain't never heard of no kid before?" Scar asked.

"You know I don't like to mix business with my personal life. I don't want him growing up in the game. I want little man to have a better life."

Scar slowly shook his head as he surveyed Day. "A'ight. Why the fuck it take you so long to come and find us?"

"I told you. I wanted to make sure the heat died down. I had no idea if y'all had gotten picked up."

"How'd you find out we didn't?" Flex asked.

"When I didn't hear nothing about it on the TV, I went out on the street and started asking niggas if they seen y'all." Day didn't look at Flex. He kept speaking to Scar.

"How we know you ain't got picked up and the feds got you doing their dirty work?" Flex said to Day then turned to Scar. "This nigga is lyin', Scar. I can feel it. He got pinched and now he workin' to put us behind bars." Flex had always been jealous of the tight relationship that Day and Scar once had. He didn't want Day coming back in and taking his place.

"You fool-ass nigga, if I was workin' for the feds or anybody, they'd be here right now." Day cut his eyes at Flex.

"You wearin' a wire then."

"Come check me." Day put his arms out to the side.

With the quickness of a cat, Flex moved in and roughly handled Day.

"Easy, nigga, before I have to beat yo' ass," Day warned.

"Fuck you. I'm checkin' for a wire, you snitch-ass bitch." Flex ripped Day's shirt open to look for the wire. The fight started immediately. Day grabbed Flex, and the two men started to wrestle. They knocked over a side table as they fell to the floor with a loud thud. Punches were landed as they fought for leverage. Day got an upper hand and started punching Flex in his face.

"Cut the bullshit!" Scar grabbed Day and easily tossed him off of Flex. Day slammed into the hallway wall as Flex struggled to his feet.

"Uncle Scar!" Talisa heard the noise and came running with her younger brother. "What is that noise?"

"It's nothing."

"Who is that?" Talisa pointed at M.J., who had silently peeked his head into the room.

"He came to play with you. His name is Malek," Day chimed in right away. His nervousness turned to excitement when he saw Derek's two kids. He was so close to his goal. Now all he needed to do was get out of there alive and call Derek.

Talisa and D.J. walked over to Malek as the adults all watched.

"Do you like trucks?" D.J. asked.

"Uh-huh." Malek nodded.

"Let's play," Talisa said. She walked into the living room with the two boys following her.

Once the children were out of sight, Scar punched Day in his stomach, knocking the wind out of him and bringing him to his knees.

"What the fuck?" Day huffed.

"That was for disappearing, nigga. While your bitch ass was hiding and dealing with yo' kid, we was tryin' to keep this business runnin'. You lucky that's all I did."

"Yeah, nigga. It was up to me, yo' ass be dead by now." Flex was standing behind Scar.

Day caught his breath and stood upright. "Look, I told you what happened. Obviously I ain't wearing no wire." He gestured to his bare chest, which had been exposed when Flex ripped open his shirt. "I'm here now and I need some work. Let's cut the bullshit."

"Nigga, you don't tell us what to do." Flex puffed his chest out.

"You think I'm gonna just give you your old spot back?" Scar asked.

As Day was about to answer, D.J. came into the room and cut him off. "We're hungry."

"Get the fuck outta here!" Scar yelled at the little boy. D.J's fear froze him. He stood staring at his uncle with watery eyes as wide as saucers. His lips started to tremble, and he started to cry as loud as only a child can.

"Damn, man. You don't gotta be like that. The kid's just hungry," Day said.

Scar snapped his head around to Day. He was obviously angry. His face was tense, and he was staring at Day like he wanted to kill him.

"Mu'fucka, you so concerned about them kids, you can take 'em. Yeah, matter of fact, that's your first job back with the organization. Take them kids until I say you finished."

Day couldn't believe his good fortune. He couldn't have dreamed it to work out any better. Instead of telling Derek where to find his children, he could now hand deliver them, reuniting with Halleigh that much sooner.

"Fine, if that's what you want. I'm willing to do whatever it takes to get back in." Initially he was going to protest, thinking that would be what Scar expected. Instead, he agreed so he could speed it up and get out of there.

"Yo, can I speak to you?" Flex said to Scar.

"Speak."

"Not in front of this shady mu'fucka." Flex gave a challenging stare to Day.

Scar gestured with a head nod for Flex to follow him to the adjoining room.

The two men spoke in hushed tones.

"We need to take care of that thing in the woods. Let's make Day dig the ditch," Flex said.

"Nah. I don't want that nigga knowing nothin' 'bout nothin' right now. Somethin' ain't right with that nigga."

"That's what I been sayin'," Flex agreed. "I don't trust that nigga."

"He gonna take them kids out my hair so we can take care of that mess out back. Then when he come back, we take care of his ass for good."

Flex couldn't hide his excitement. "Finally. I been thinkin' that nigga need to get murked for a minute."

"Get ready to be diggin' two graves tonight, son."

"No doubt. I'll dig that mu'fucka's grave myself." Flex was smiling from ear to ear.

Even though he wanted to take the kids and leave, Day waited patiently for the two men to return. He didn't want to stir up any more suspicion, so he was going to let them dictate how this meeting would go.

"All good?" Day asked as the two men returned from their private meeting.

"As long as you take them kids out my hair, yeah, it's all good."

"Like I said, whatever you need me to do, boss."

"Good. Take them kids and come back tomorrow night."

Day gathered up the kids as fast as he could. They were having fun playing together, so they were somewhat resistant to the idea of leaving. When Day bribed them with a trip to Dave and Buster's, they were quick to jump in the car.

"Sayonara, mu'fucka. Enjoy your last day on the planet." Scar stood in the window and watched as Day drove away with the kids.

Once out of sight of the house, Day called Derek.

"I know where your kids are," he said.

"Tell me."

"They in the backseat of my car."

"Let me speak to them." Derek's heart was beating fast.

"Let me speak to Halleigh," Day countered.

Derek didn't want to tell him that he had released her. "Trust me, she's safe."

"Trust me. I got your kids. Meet me in two hours."

Day gave Derek the address of Halleigh's house and hung up the phone.

"Shit," Derek said to himself. He was now regretting letting Halleigh free. For all he knew, she could have made it home by now. If Day got home to see Halleigh, Derek's chances of rescuing his children could be in jeopardy.

Derek grabbed his gun, jumped in his car, and sped toward a hopeful reunion with his children. He had no idea what he was going to do once he met with Day, but he was prepared to do whatever it took to keep his children safe.

Chapter 15

Painful Reunion

Derek arrived at Halleigh's house well within the two-hour timeframe Dayvid had given him. He parked in his usual spot around the corner and out of sight of the house. He proceeded to his hiding place in the woods and began his wait for Dayvid—and hopefully his children.

As he sat there in the cover of the trees, he thought about his strategy. How could he stall Day and reclaim his children? His bargaining chip was Halleigh, and he had let her go. Now he had nothing. He didn't know what he was going to do. His strategy was going to be to wait, see what Day did, then react. He sat in nervous anticipation as he carefully watched the house.

This could be the end of a long nightmare, he thought as he leaned up against a tree trunk. He vowed to himself that when he got his children back, he would get as far away from Baltimore as possible. He was tired of living his life always searching for retribution. He was going to devote his life to his children and raising them to be trustworthy, responsible adults.

The sound of the garage door opening and Day pulling in pulled Derek from his thoughts. He watched the garage door slowly close as he stood and positioned his gun in his waistband for easy retrieval. He took a deep breath and prepared himself for the showdown.

He pulled out his cell phone and redialed the number Day had called him from.

"Welcome home," Derek said after Day had answered. He could hear the children in the background, talking to one another. "Now, bring my kids outside."

"The fuck make you think you callin' the shots, nigga?" Day drew his gun while he peeked out the window, looking for Derek. "Let me speak to Halleigh."

"You don't speak to her until I see my children."

"Let me see you. Come to the front of the driveway."

Derek followed orders and came out from the corner of the house. He stood at the end of the driveway and raised his arms like Jesus on the cross. He knew he was taking a chance and that Day could shoot him, but he gambled, thinking that Day wouldn't do anything until he saw Halleigh.

Derek put his phone to his ear. "You satisfied?"

"Where is she?"

"Come outside." Derek hung up.

Day was hesitant. He didn't have a good feeling about this situation. Not seeing Halleigh had him concerned. He was starting to think that Derek might be playing him. Before going outside, he ushered the children upstairs into Malek's room.

"Y'all stay up here and play. If you good, we can go to the toy store later."

The children's eyes lit up and smiles stretched across their faces. They were already thinking about the toys they would buy. There was no way they were going to ruin their chance to get new toys.

Day looked out all of the windows of the house to make sure there was no ambush about to happen. He slowly opened the door and walked onto the front lawn. When Derek saw Day, he slowly walked toward him.

"That's far enough," Day said, keeping a safe distance between himself and Derek.

The two men were now face to face, each man at opposite ends of the yard, like an old Western showdown at high noon. The question was, who would be the first to flinch?

"This has gone on long enough. Let's end this now. Bring my kids outside."

"Nigga, you think it's that easy? You ain't gettin' shit until I see Halleigh," Day said.

"I guess we have a standoff then, because I'm not bringing Halleigh until I see my kids."

"Let me speak to her."

"No," Derek answered.

Day was becoming frustrated. He was getting the feeling that Halleigh was dead. *Why else won't he let me speak to her?* Day thought.

"Look, let me speak to her and this can all be over," Day said.

"She doesn't have a phone."

"Then let me see her. Take me to her."

"If you give me my kids, then I'll tell you where she is."

The situation was becoming heated. With each passing second, both men were becoming increasingly more agitated. Derek didn't know how much longer he could hold Day off, and Day was losing hope that Halleigh was alive. Something needed to give. This game couldn't go on any longer. It was just a matter of who would make the first move.

Derek felt like he was running out of time. He thought Day would figure it out sooner or later, so he needed to make things happen. His children needed him and he needed them. He started walking toward the front door.

"Stay put, nigga. I'm warning you." Day positioned himself between Derek and the door. Derek hesitated for a second then resumed his march.

"Stop, mu'fucka."

Derek didn't listen. He felt his only shot was to call Day's bluff and fight his way through the door. Derek took two more steps, and Day reached in his waistband for his gun. Derek saw this movement and did the same. Shots came firing out of both guns as each man attempted to dodge the flying bullets.

It was seconds of chaos, then complete silence. Both men lay still on the grass; each had been hit. Derek felt a sharp pain in his right shoulder. He reached over with his left hand and winced in pain as he touched the hole where the bullet had pierced him.

With a bullet lodged in his shoulder, picking himself up off the grass was difficult. He had minimal use of his right arm. Keeping an eye on Day the entire time, he got up and cautiously walked over to check on Day, who hadn't moved yet.

Blood had saturated Day's shirt. His mouth hung open, with a small bloodstream trickling out of it and down his cheek. It appeared to Derek that he had hit Day in the abdomen and chest.

Derek shook his head. He hadn't wanted it to end like this. He just wanted peace. He didn't want to kill anyone. Derek regretted lying to Day. He regretted getting caught up in his brother's crimes. If he had told the truth to Day, maybe this wouldn't have turned out like this.

As he was bending down to pick up Day's gun and check his pulse, a car came speeding down the street.

Derek swiveled around and pointed both guns at the oncoming car. The car screeched to a halt in front of the house and the passenger's side door flung open. Derek kept his guns aimed, his right shoulder burning in pain.

Halleigh jumped out and ran to Derek. As she got closer, she realized that Day was on the ground, covered in blood.

Seeing Derek with a gun, the guy driving the car sped off before Halleigh had barely exited the car. He didn't even wait for her to close the door. He just reached over while he sped off and closed it himself. He had some warrants out and wasn't about to get caught up in whatever bullshit was happening. He had just picked Halleigh up while she was hitchhiking, hoping that for his good deed she would let him get a little piece.

"What did you do?" she screamed.

Derek lowered his gun. "It's not what you think."

Halleigh dropped to her knees beside Day. She grabbed his shoulders and started shaking him. "Wake up! Dayvid! Wake up! It's me! It's Halleigh!" Tears were streaming down her face. This was not the reunion she had been envisioning. She was supposed to come and surprise Day then profess her love for him. They were supposed to make passionate love, get married, and live happily ever after.

She cradled his face in both hands, and through her sobs she spoke to him. "I love you. You can't leave me. Do not leave me. You hear?"

Day's body was limp. He wasn't responding to Halleigh's pleas. Derek stood there not knowing what to do. He wanted to help Halleigh and ease her pain, but he was the one responsible for her pain. He felt ashamed and useless.

With her hands covered in blood, Halleigh jumped up and started hitting Derek in the chest as hard as she could. She was a wild beast attacking her prey.

"What have you done? What have you done?" she screamed over and over as she continued to pound on Derek's chest. He feebly tried to protect himself from her blows, but felt that he deserved the punishment he was getting.

She continued throwing punches until she had spent all of her energy and could barely lift her arms. Her arms hurt from punching, her head hurt from crying, and her heart hurt from all the pain she had gone through in her life. She wanted to end it all right there. She had lost all hope. She saw no reason to keep on living. Life was too hard and only filled with disappointment.

"I can't do this anymore," she sobbed. "It's too much. It's too hard." She reached for Derek's gun.

"Whoa." He pulled the gun away. "What are you talking about? What about your son? You need to stay strong for him."

"Why?" Halleigh asked. "It's no use. He's just going to learn that life is one big 'fuck you' then you die."

"Don't say that. You're a fighter. When I kidnapped you, did you give up? No. Why? Because you were fighting for your son so you could be there for him and give him the stable and safe life you never had."

Halleigh wiped tears from her face. Derek's words had broken through to her, but she still wasn't convinced that she shouldn't just end it all.

"I don't even know where Malek is. I give up." Her body was tired and weak. She stared at her feet as her head hung down.

"He's in the house. He needs you."

Halleigh looked up. Hearing that Malek was so close gave her a sudden burst of energy and excitement. "He is?" Her hopelessness instantly turned to hope. Without thinking, she ran to the house. She took the stairs two at a time. She couldn't get to her son fast enough. She burst through the door and saw Malek and two other children huddled in the corner.

"Mama!" Malek jumped up and ran to her. Halleigh scooped him up in her arms and squeezed her little boy as tightly as she could. She planted kisses all over his face and head.

"Daddy!" D.J. and Talisa yelled in unison. Derek had come running up behind Halleigh. He dropped to his knees when he saw his children, and they came crashing into him. It was the family reunion Derek had been dreaming about. He started crying the second he saw his two beautiful children.

"Mama. Why are you bleeding?"

In her haste, Halleigh had forgotten that her hands were covered in blood.

"You too, Daddy." Talisa pointed at her father's chest.

"Ah, we were trying to help a man that was hurt. We're all right. We'll get cleaned up later." Derek deflected the question. "Halleigh, can I speak to you?"

She didn't want to let go of Malek, but she relented and met Derek in the hallway just outside of Malek's room.

"I'm getting far away from Baltimore. I suggest you do the same."

"Where am I supposed to go? I can't go back to Flint." Halleigh had left the memories and hardship of Flint behind and had nothing to go back to. She figured it would be a dead end going back to the city where all of her heartbreak had started. She wanted a new life, and going back to Flint would be a step in the wrong direction.

"Do you have any family anywhere? Out west? Down south?"

"I think I have a cousin in Little Rock."

"Then go there."

Halleigh thought about it for a minute. "Okay. I'll pack up and head out tomorrow."

"No. You have to get out of here now. It's too dangerous for you in Baltimore. The police will be here asking questions. You have to go right now. No time to waste."

It took no time for Halleigh to realize that Derek was right. She needed to get as far away from Baltimore as she could.

"Malek, come here, baby." He came running. "Tell your friends good-bye. We're going to visit cousins in Little Rock."

Usually Malek would put up a fight before leaving his friends, but since he hadn't seen his mama in so long, he was eager to spend time with her. He clung to his mother's leg and said his good-byes.

"Take him through the garage. He doesn't need to see out front," Derek whispered to Halleigh.

Halleigh picked up Malek and ran down the stairs into the garage. A few seconds later she came rushing back into the house.

"I need the keys to the truck."

They quickly searched the house and couldn't find them.

"They must be on Day. I'll get them. You wait in the truck," Derek said.

Outside, Derek knelt down and went to reach in Day's pocket. As he put his hand inside the front pock-

et, Day grabbed Derek's ankle. Derek jumped back and
fell onto his ass. "What the . . . ?"

"Shoot me," Day said barely above a whisper.

"You're alive?" Derek was in shock.

"Shoot me." Day barely had enough strength to turn
his head to face Derek.

Derek ignored him and went back to rummaging
through his pockets. He found the keys and ran back
into the house.

"Here. Now, go. Don't look at the front yard when
you back up. Just go. You don't need to see that again."

Halleigh took the keys. She started the truck and
backed out of the garage. Even though she desperately
wanted to look one last time, she followed Derek's directions and averted her eyes from the body lying on
the lawn.

Day heard the garage door open and struggled to
move enough to see his truck backing out. As the truck
reversed out of the driveway, he could see Halleigh
through the windshield.

"Halleigh," he called out breathlessly. She wasn't going to hear his whisper.

He tried again to summon the breath to make his
voice loud enough for her to hear. The bullet had
punctured his lung, making it too difficult for him to
gain any force behind his words. "Halleigh. Wait," he
whispered as his head fell back and he stared up into
the sky.

Derek waited until Halleigh was out of sight then
went back out to Day. Day was lying there with his eyes
closed. When he sensed someone standing over him,
he slowly opened them.

"Kill me," he whispered when he saw Derek. He was
in excruciating pain and was barely able to breathe.
"Please."

"I'm not killing anyone. There has been enough murder already."

Day struggled to get his words out. "Please. Put me out of my misery. I have nothing left."

"I won't shoot you. No doubt the police are on their way. You can decide your fate before they get here."

"I'm begging."

Derek walked away, but stopped after a few steps. "I won't kill you, but you can decide what to do before anyone gets here." Derek dropped one of the guns on the ground and proceeded back into the house.

He gathered his children and ushered them out the back door, through the woods, and to his car. He buckled them in and drove away from the curb, happy to have his children back where they belonged.

"Who likes the beach?"

"Me!" Both children raised their hands.

"Who wants to live on the beach?"

"Me!" They raised their hands again and waved them wildly.

"Good, because we're moving to California."

Day stared at the gun a few feet from him. He summoned up the strength to roll over onto his stomach. After taking a few seconds to recover from the exertion and the pain, he began crawling on his stomach toward the gun. It was taking every ounce of strength and will for him to crawl. With every inch he moved, he was leaving a trail of blood behind him.

Unable to crawl any farther, he collapsed. He stretched out his arm to the gun. His fingertips were millimeters from touching it. With one last burst of energy, he lunged and grabbed the gun. In agonizing pain, he rolled over onto his back. He took the gun in both hands and placed the barrel in his mouth.

Day heard sirens in the distance. He closed his eyes and said a prayer. He thought about Halleigh and M.J. one last time. The sirens were getting closer. Day finished his prayer, thought to himself, *I love you, Halleigh,* and pulled the trigger. The gun dropped onto his chest. Day was gone.

The EMT didn't even bother trying to resuscitate him. With his face blown off, it was obvious to them that Day was dead. They loaded him into the back of the ambulance and quietly pulled away from the house as detectives began knocking on doors to question neighbors about what they'd seen.

Chapter 16

Sneak Attack

The sun still hadn't risen in the east as Flex patted the dirt with the back of the shovel to flatten it out. It was the final patch of dirt to be smoothed over the makeshift grave they had dug. He and Scar had been in the woods all night, burying Arnold.

Even though both men were out there, Flex had done most of the work. Needless to say, this did not sit well with Flex, but he kept his mouth shut and just kept digging. He had a good mind to whack the shit out of Scar with his shovel every time Scar would take a break and make Flex keep on digging.

"That should do it," Flex said.

"You stupid? Cover that shit with leaves 'n sticks 'n shit," Scar said in a condescending tone.

"We in the middle of nowhere. No one's gonna see this." Flex gave Scar a dose of his own attitude.

"You a dumb mu'fucka, you know that? That snoopy-ass wife come out here and see fresh dug earth, you don't think she gonna start digging?"

"I shoulda had her ass out here digging tonight. Woulda had this shit done a lot sooner. Sure she woulda helped more than your ass did."

"What the fuck you just say?" Scar made a move toward Flex. He stepped on the grave, and his foot sank into the dirt up to his ankle. "Fuck. Now I got dirt all in my shoe." He stopped his attack as he got distracted and pulled his foot free.

Flex started laughing when Scar pulled his dirt-covered foot from the ground. "Oh shit. That's funny." He pointed.

"Mu'fucka, you best watch what you say," Scar warned as he took off his boot and shook out the dirt.

"You right. I'm tired. It's been a long night. That shit was wrong." Flex's words said he apologized, but inside he was still telling Scar to fuck off.

"Damn right it was wrong. You eat because of me. I'll take that away just as easy as I gave it to you. I may be layin' my head in the country, but I still run B-More," Scar said.

Flex paused for a second, stared at Scar, then said, "You right." Flex started spreading leaves over the grave. As he did this, he thought, *You may run B-More now, but your time is coming to an end. It's time for a new regime, a new king.*

The two men walked back to the house in silence. Each man had a feeling that something was not right. The stress of their situation was tearing them apart. There was a power struggle beginning, and neither one was going to give in. Scar wasn't going to let some young upstart try to muscle his way into his seat, and Flex wasn't going to allow an old has-been to continue to keep him down.

They walked side by side so they could keep an eye on each other. Each man thought that if the other got behind him, it would surely mean a shovel to the back of the head.

"Leave the shovel outside," Scar instructed as they reached the house.

"A'ight. We still gotta clean up the basement."

"Nah. You take Charisma home and get some rest. I'll take care of the blood downstairs."

"You sure?" Flex was confused. He thought for sure that Scar would make him go directly down to the basement and clean up Arnold's blood.

"I'm sure. I'll take care of it. You did good work tonight. Get some rest and we can start fresh tomorrow." Scar just wanted Flex out of his sight for a while. He thought that maybe the fact that they had been up for so long was the reason they were getting on each other's nerves.

"A'ight," Flex answered. "Yo, Charisma. Get yo' ass up. We leavin'," he yelled up the stairs. After waiting a few seconds and not hearing anything moving upstairs, he ascended the steps.

Charisma was still asleep when Flex entered the room. He shook her to wake her from her slumber. "Let's go."

She rubbed her eyes and stretched her body to work out the kinks. "What you want?"

"It's time to leave."

"Good. I'm g'tting bored out here."

Flex and Charisma walked downstairs together. They were both in a hurry to get back to the city. Charisma wanted to get back to hang with her girls, and Flex needed to start lining up soldiers.

"Yo, we out." Flex walked past Scar without even stopping.

Scar said nothing in return. He stayed silent as he sat at the kitchen table with the pile of money in front of him.

Flex pulled out of the driveway as fast as he could. He needed to get back to his crib, lay his head, and get some shut-eye. The sun was just peeking over the horizon as he and Charisma drove the winding country roads.

Not even a mile from Scar's house, as Flex steered the car around a long, lazy curve, flashing blue and red lights came from the opposite direction. The police caravan came speeding around the corner. There was every variety of cop car Flex could imagine: vans, SUVs, cruisers, unmarked cars. Flex was certain that it wasn't just local cops, either. The unmarked cars looked too new and nice to be some small-town cop cars. Those were federal cars, most likely DEA, FBI, or both. Flex had a good idea where they were heading.

After the cars were around the corner, Flex took out his cell phone. Just as he was about to push the button to call Scar and warn him, he had a change of heart. He stopped himself from making the call and put the phone back in his pocket.

Fuck him. Nigga can fend for his self.

"What was that?" Charisma asked.

"Mind yo' business."

They drove the rest of the way to Baltimore in silence.

Scar was still sitting at the kitchen table when he heard a car come speeding up his driveway.

What this dumb mu'fucka forget now? He trippin' if he think I'm givin' him any more cash.

He looked over to the window next to the front door and saw the flashing lights shining through. "Fuck!" He jumped up and ran up to his bedroom, taking the stairs two at a time. He dove under his bed and grabbed his AK-47, then went to his closet and pulled out the fake wall in the back. Behind the wall was an armory of weapons: shotguns, Uzis, handguns, and enough bullets for a war. He armed himself with every weapon he could handle.

Running to the second floor window that overlooked the front door, Scar began loading his weapons. When he looked out the window, he saw dozens of officers exiting their cars and fanning out on his property.

Four officers crouching down with their guns drawn started toward the front door. Before they had a chance to get there, Scar let his AK sing. The window shattered as the bullets pierced the glass and made their way directly to the four officers. Scar easily took the men out. They were down before they knew what was going on.

Scar's gunfire triggered a reaction from the dozens of other officers. They opened fire on the house with abandon. Bullets smashed out windows, lodged into the side of the house, and sent splinters of wood flying in all directions. Scar hit the ground as soon as the officers opened fire.

When the melee quieted down, Scar jumped up and returned fire, causing the officers to take cover. As he was firing out the front window, he heard the back door get smashed in. He ran to the top of the stairs, and as soon as he saw an officer, he opened fire again.

He drained his AK of its bullets and threw it off to the side. He grabbed his shotgun and began blasting down the stairs. After emptying the shotgun, he ran back to the front window and opened up with his Uzi.

"You mu'fuckas ain't no match for me!" he screamed down to the officers as the bullets sprayed wildly.

As he spewed bullets all over the front yard, a flash bomb came crashing through the window behind Scar. It detonated before Scar could throw it back. It stunned Scar and sent him crashing to the ground. Directly following the flash bomb, a smoke bomb hit the floor and filled the room with smoke.

Scar gained his composure and, through the smoke, started randomly firing at the door to the room. He emptied the clip and started reloading.

As soon as there was a lull in his gunfire, officers stormed into the room. They pounced on top of Scar like a football team diving for a fumble. There was a pile of bodies on top of Scar. Arms and legs were flailing as all the officers either reached for Scar's guns or tried to get their shots in.

"Get the fuck off me!" Scar roared.

"Stay down. Don't move!" Several of the officers were yelling.

Scar ignored their warnings and continued to fight. They were gouging his eyes, punching his kidneys, and bending back his fingers, but Scar still tried to scurry away. He fought a valiant fight, but the number of officers was too overwhelming for him.

The officers subdued Scar and cuffed his wrists and ankles.

"Scar Johnson, you are under arrest."

"Y'all ain't got nothin' on me."

"We have enough evidence to put you away for life. I'm sure once we go through this place, we will find even more crimes we can charge you with."

Scar immediately thought about the blood in the basement that he hadn't cleaned up. *Fuck!*

As the officer read him his Miranda rights and went through the list of charges, Scar stopped listening. He just sat on the floor in the middle of the room, staring out the back window. He was caught, and he didn't have Tiphani to bail him out this time. He thought about his brother, Derek, and his mother, and all the foster homes he had been through.

As he reminisced, a black bird flew onto the windowsill. Scar and the bird stared at one another. Scar's only thought was: *Mu'fuckin' birds! I hate the fuckin' country.*

Chapter 17

Fall from Grace

The gavel came down with a thud. Mathias Steele sat there in shock. He had just been sentenced to life without parole for the attempted murder of the governor. How had he fallen so far so fast? It seemed like yesterday to him that he ruled Baltimore. He had every criminal paying him off, he had all the other politicians scared, and he could do whatever he pleased. Now he was headed to a maximum security prison.

"What now?" Mathias asked his attorney.

"They take you to prison. I'm sorry. We will fight this."

"I'm going to a white collar prison, right?"

The attorney shook his head. "I tried, but unfortunately you made a lot of enemies, and no one was willing to cut you a break. You're going to max. General population." His tone was sympathetic.

The court officers came to handcuff Mathias and lead him back to the bowels of the courthouse. They began the process of transporting him to his new home behind bars.

Mathias was forcing down the shitty food in the chow hall. He had been in the prison for a day and was miserable. He was fiending to get high, his body ached and itched all over, and his cellie was a huge Mexican dude who snored all night. It was his worst nightmare come true.

As he stared into the slop on his plate, three big, bald dudes surrounded him. The biggest of the bunch sat to his left.

"You new in here."

Mathias didn't look up from his plate and refused to say anything.

"You the mayor who a crackhead now, right?"

Mathias remained quiet. The big dude discreetly punched him in the ribs so the C.O. wouldn't see. "I asked you a question."

Mathias grimaced "Yes. That's me."

"Was that so hard? I'm Blade."

"Nice to meet you," Mathias begrudgingly answered but still wouldn't look at the man.

"You need anything in here, I'm your man."

This finally caught Mathias's interest, and he turned to look at the hulking six foot six monster of a man. "You get me high?"

"You gonna suck my dick?"

"What?"

"You wanna get high, you gonna have to suck my dick," Blade said.

"Fuck that." Mathias went back to eating.

"Nigga, you will be suckin' my dick. Believe that. Watch yo' back." Blade took another shot at Mathias's ribs as he got up from the table. The three men strode through the chow hall with confidence. They were obviously feared men in this prison.

Mathias was walking through the common room back to his cell. Even though he was now one of them, he still had his air of superiority and felt he was better than the rest of the convicts. He had no desire to hang with any of the common criminals he was surrounded by. He preferred to spend his time alone in his cell.

One of the men who had surrounded him earlier got up from a bench across the room and started toward him. The dude had his right hand cupped around a shank. Mathias saw this and turned in the opposite direction. The man picked up his pace and Mathias did the same. Mathias headed back toward the chow hall. As he turned a corner, he ran into a C.O.

"Where are you going?" the C.O. asked.

"To my cell."

The prisoner chasing Mathias saw him speaking with the guard and stopped his pursuit. He covered the shank and turned on his heels in the opposite direction.

"Wrong way, prisoner. This is the chow hall."

"I'm sorry, sir. This is my first day here. I'm all turned around."

"I'll take you there. That inmate looked like he wanted a piece of you."

Mathias was relieved to get an escort back to his cell. Little did he know that it was probably the worst decision he could have made. As he walked through the prison with the guard, all the other inmates saw him. He was immediately labeled as a friend of the guards and a snitch. He made enemies on the inside that he didn't even know he had.

That night, he got the beating of his life. Around two in the morning, his cell door opened. Blade had bribed the guards. He wanted to show Mathias who was boss. A dozen inmates were standing outside his cell, waiting for their chance to beat on the snitch.

Mathias was barely able to open his eyes before the first blow connected to his face. Growing up privileged, Mathias had never been in a fistfight. He had no idea what to do to defend himself, so most of the inmates were getting clean shots. They were relentless, and with Blade's encouragement, it made the inmates even more violent. Punch after punch connected with Mathias's body. Whenever he covered one part of his body, the inmates would focus on another. After a while, Mathias just passed out, yet the inmates still continued their attack. They were like a pack of wolves attacking a carcass. When it was all said and done, Mathias was beaten to within an inch of his life. He spent the next month in the infirmary.

After they found the blood in the basement at Scar's hideout, the authorities scanned the surrounding area and found the makeshift grave where Arnold was buried. Betsy was relieved to have found her husband's body to be able to give him a proper burial. It was a beautiful ceremony for a kind, warmhearted, caring man that left this earth much too soon.

Now Betsy sat in the front row of the courthouse as the verdict was read. She wanted to be there when they put the man responsible for her husband's death behind bars.

"On the charge of first degree murder, we, the jury, find the defendant guilty."

A buzz went through the courtroom. Betsy wept openly and hugged the prosecutor. There were other charges being read, but Betsy didn't listen. The murder charge was the only one she was interested in.

Even though she felt some satisfaction that Scar would be going away for life, she wasn't comforted. She would always have a hole in her heart. She would never get her husband back.

"I hope you rot in hell!" She jumped up from the court bench as Scar was being led out. He didn't even turn. He kept shuffling along with the court officers.

The judge banged his gavel. "Order!"

The attorney grabbed Betsy's shoulders to calm her down. He escorted her out the front and away from Scar.

After being processed and admitted, Scar walked through the common room with his prison-issued items. Inmates stopped what they were doing and watched as the famous Scar Johnson walked by. Each one was sizing him up, scheming to be the first one to take him down and make a name for himself.

When Scar got to his cell, there was a skinny little dude lying on the bottom bunk. Scar stood in the doorway and stared at the dude.

"Oh, hey. You my new cellie?" the effeminate man said.

"Get the fuck up. You on my cot, punk," Scar said menacingly.

"Uh-uh. This my bunk. You're on top."

Scar dropped his things and grabbed the dude out of the bunk. "Mu'fuckin' faggot. I said this my bunk." He pushed the dude out the cell door.

"You done fucked up." The effeminate man ran away.

Scar stripped the bed of the guy's sheets and put on his own sheets. Satisfied that he had asserted his dominance over his cellie, he lay down on the bed.

About fifteen minutes later, Blade entered Scar's cell with two men behind him. They picked Scar up off the bunk and went to town. They threw him to the ground and began the beating. Kicks were slamming into every part of Scar's body.

Scar was taken by surprise, but he put up a good fight. He grabbed one dude's foot and pulled him to the ground. He struggled to get on top of the inmate and started slamming his fist into the guy's face.

It didn't last long, as the other two pulled Scar off their friend. They pinned Scar down and focused all their anger on his head. Fists and feet rained down. Scar got in a couple more good shots, but in the end the three hulking men overpowered him. Scar was in a fetal position on the floor, covering up as best he could as they kicked him like a soccer ball.

"Don't ever call my bitch a faggot. You respect my bitch. Yo' ass sleeps on the top bunk," Blade commanded as he gave Scar one last kick to the ribs and walked out.

Scar's cellie came prancing in. "I told you, you fucked up." He stripped the bottom bunk of Scar's sheets and threw them on top of Scar. "And you can make my bunk up for me." Then he pranced back out of the cell.

Five minutes later, Scar had picked himself off of the floor and was sitting on the toilet. He was wiping blood from his mouth when Mathias appeared at his cell.

"Looks like you got a nice welcome. You deserve it," Mathias said.

"Fuck you." Scar snapped his head up to see who was mocking him. He was shocked to see the former mayor of Baltimore standing in his cell. It was even more shocking that he was wearing prison-issued clothing.

"The fuck you in for?" Scar asked.

"I tried to kill the governor."

"Oh shit. You a killer now," Scar mocked. He looked at Mathias and saw all the bruises and scars on his face. "Looks like you got worked over pretty good yo'self."

"I did. That's why I'm standing here right now."

"If you don't get out my face, I'll work yo' ass over too."

"Hold up. We need each other in here."

"The fuck you mean?" Scar spit blood through his legs and into the toilet.

These two men had been adversaries, battling for control of Baltimore. Scar had wanted this man dead and vice versa. Now Mathias was proposing they work together. Scar didn't trust Mathias's intentions.

"After I got worked over, I was in the infirmary for a while. I made some friends up there. I can get my hands on any painkiller I want." Mathias raised his eyebrows.

"I don't fuck with that shit."

"You aren't hearing me. You are a marked man in here. Everyone is going to take their shot at the big, bad Scar Johnson. If we work together, I could hold some of my clients off for a while."

"I don't need yo' protection," Scar said.

"No, you don't, but I need yours. I will cut you in on my business if you take out that bastard Blade. He's the one that just kicked your ass and the one responsible for landing me in the sick bay. I want that motherfucker dead. You take him out, you become head nigga, and we could run this place—you, the muscle, and me, the supplier. We split it fifty-fifty."

Scar thought about the proposal for a second. He couldn't believe how far they had fallen. They were once kings of Baltimore, and now they were fighting for their existence in a federal pen. He was surprised at the turn of events in his life.

"Fuck it. I'm in here for life. Might as well." Scar stood and shook Mathias's hand. "Now, let's get to planning. I wanna be runnin' this joint by the end of the week."

Chapter 17

Different Faces, Same Old Story

Cecil sat in the driver's seat of his sedan, staring intently at the front door of the bank in downtown Baltimore. He watched customers and employees walking in and out during a typical workday afternoon. The guard stood at the front door, oblivious to Cecil's peering eyes. He was too busy daydreaming about relaxing and fishing on his new boat when his retirement began in two months.

Cecil was getting anxious. He had been sitting there too long. His plan was to get in and out; it had already been forty-five minutes. Something needed to happen. The inactivity was making him uneasy.

Just as he was preparing to get out of the car and go into the bank, Cecil saw the manager go up to the guard, say something, and point to Cecil's car. Cecil stayed put, but he discreetly reached for his gun and placed it on the seat between his legs. He didn't like that they were aware of him. He was supposed to remain anonymous during this scam, and to protect his identity, he was willing to do whatever it took.

The guard and the manager looked at the car and then walked away from the door. Cecil thought about driving away, but he decided to stay put and wait out the situation.

The manager came back into view and opened the front door so the guard could walk through. A young woman dressed in business attire and carrying a large duffel bag followed the guard. The guard stopped just outside the door, surveyed the situation, and then escorted the woman toward Cecil's car. Cecil watched all of this transpiring and cocked his gun as the guard got closer to his vehicle.

The guard stopped at Cecil's car and, same as before, he surveyed the surrounding area. The woman he was escorting walked up to the rear passenger's door and opened it. Like a longshoreman throwing a sack of potatoes, she heaved the duffel bag into the back seat and slammed the door shut.

Cecil had a fleeting thought to throw the car into gear and speed off. Before he was able to turn on the car and do that, the woman opened the passenger's side door and got in the car.

"Got it, baby." She smiled.

"What's with the guard?"

"They wanted to escort me. Said it made them more comfortable." She shrugged her shoulders.

The guard tapped on the window. The woman opened the window.

"You take care—and be careful with all of that." The guard motioned with his head toward the backseat.

"We will," responded Cecil. He pressed the button to make the window close then started the car and drove away from the curb, leaving the guard to watch them drive down the street.

"What took so long?" Cecil asked.

"They insisted on counting it all out. It took a while. That's a lot of money," she answered.

"I started to think you dipped out the back door."

"Babe, you know I would never do that to you," the woman said.

Cecil had met the woman one day when he went into a coffee shop to grab some lunch. She had commented on how attractive Cecil's mismatched eyes were. Her comment sparked a conversation, and Cecil persuaded her to take a break and sit with him. He learned her name was Brooke and she was working her way through college at the coffee shop.

"How old are you, Brooke?" Cecil had asked as he sipped his coffee.

"I'm twenty-one," she said with the pride of someone who'd recently turned that pivotal age.

"What are you studying?"

"I want to be a teacher, but I don't know if I'll make it."

"What do you mean?"

"This job doesn't exactly make me rich. I'm behind on my tuition and may have to drop out."

Cecil and Brooke had continued to talk until her break was over. They exchanged phone numbers and planned to meet later that evening.

Cecil had left the coffee shop with a little bounce in his step. He felt that fate had intervened and he had met the perfect woman for his plan. He needed a woman to help him retrieve Tiphani's money from her offshore accounts. Brooke seemed to fit everything he was looking for—smart, respectable-looking, in need of money, and just gullible enough to not question him.

They had met that night and slept together, and then continued to sleep together every night for the next week. One night, while they lay in bed, Cecil proposed his idea to Brooke. She would call the bank overseas, he would provide her with all the information she needed, and then she would go to the bank and retrieve the cash. "Easy," he'd said. He would, of course, pay for her tuition and spending money.

Brooke hadn't thought twice about it. She trusted Cecil, and the thought of having her tuition paid made the decision even easier.

"What now?" Brooke asked as they drove down the highway with the bag of money.

"I don't know. Let's take a road trip."

"Okay, but I need to go home and get some clothes," Brooke said excitedly.

"We have five million in cash in the back seat. We can buy you whatever you need."

"That sounds better." She smiled from ear to ear.

Cecil wasn't planning on taking a road trip. He was planning on leaving and never coming back. He had been in Baltimore too long. He hated the city and wanted to leave as soon as possible. To Cecil, it felt like the Wild West. He wasn't without sin, but he expected a certain amount of loyalty from people and he saw none in Baltimore. Everyone was all about themselves—except Brooke.

About an hour into the trip, Cecil pulled into a rest area with a visitors' center. There was one car in the parking lot, presumably owned by the person who worked at the visitors' center.

"What are we doing?" asked Brooke.

"Need to stretch my legs."

"Okay. I need to pee anyway." She unfastened her seatbelt and exited the car. Cecil did the same and made sure to bring his gun. He followed Brooke as she walked to the bathroom in the back of the building.

Cecil now had a decision to make. He hated leaving witnesses who'd had any contact with him, but he liked

Brooke. She was a sweet girl who wasn't trying to harm anyone.

Does she live or does she die? Cecil pulled out his gun and hid it behind his back as he closed the gap between them. Brooke heard footsteps coming up behind her as she reached the bathroom door. She quickly turned around.

"Babe, what are you doing?" She was relieved that the footsteps belonged to Cecil.

"Making sure you're safe."

"Thanks. I'm fine." She leaned in and gave him a peck on the cheek. "Can you go inside the visitors' center and see if they have any snacks?"

Cecil discreetly put the gun back in his waistband. "Of course."

They parted ways.

Brooke walked back to the car after she finished up in the bathroom. She was in a good mood. The stress she felt from school and work had disappeared for the first time in a long time. She was excited about the impromptu road trip. She didn't care where they went; she was just happy to be getting away for a while.

When she turned the corner and faced the parking lot, she stopped dead in her tracks. She was confused by what she saw—or actually, what she didn't see. Cecil's car had disappeared. She ran to the visitors' center to alert Cecil that his car was stolen. She frantically pushed through the door and ran to the first person she saw, the little old man sitting behind the desk.

"Where is my boyfriend?" she blurted out with wild eyes.

"Haven't seen him. In fact, I haven't seen anyone in about an hour. I'm about to close up."

"Tall black guy, one blue eye, one brown. He didn't come in here?"

"Nope."

Brooke ran back outside and ran around the parking lot. She searched in every direction, but she saw nothing. Stopping in the middle of the parking lot, she slowly turned in a circle. She didn't understand what was happening. Where was Cecil? Where was his car?

The sun had set, and the parking lot lit up as the lights flickered on overhead. Brooke looked at the empty parking space where the car had been parked. This time, she noticed something on the ground. As she approached the object, she saw that it was the duffel bag that held the money. On top of the bag was a slip of paper with her name scribbled on it.

She was hoping it was a note from Cecil, some sort of explanation, but her hopes were dashed when she picked up the paper and saw the rest was blank. The bag wasn't full, but there were several stacks of cash left inside. Brooke counted the stacks. It was two hundred thousand dollars.

The little old man came from the visitors' center. "Did you find him?" he called across the lot. Brooke quickly stuffed the stack she was holding back into the bag.

"No. He left me."

The man came closer. "I'm sorry. I can give you a ride to the bus or train if you want."

"That would be great. Thank you."

Cecil was well on his way down the highway. When Brooke had turned around at the visitors' center and Cecil looked into her innocent eyes, he couldn't bring himself to kill her. He liked Brooke and wanted her to keep her innocence for as long as she could. That was why he decided to leave her. He didn't want her getting mixed up in his shady life, and he figured he was better off alone. He left her enough money to pay for her tuition, plus she wouldn't have to work for the rest of her time in school.

Cecil watched the road in front of him. There was no looking back. He was on to the next city, destination unknown.

In another slightly different visitors' center, a young corner boy sat slumped in a chair. He had a scowl on his face and on his head sat a Ravens cap. He tugged at his baggy jeans as he waited for the man he was visiting.

The door at the end of the long row of visiting booths opened up, and the boy sat up straighter. He kept the scowl, though. Scar sauntered into the room.

The guards directed Scar to the booth where the boy was sitting. Scar sat across from the boy and picked up the phone so he could hear his visitor on the other side of the plexiglass. The boy did the same.

Scar's face was bruised and swollen. It looked to the boy like he had been freshly beaten. In fact, he had. Scar's plan to take over the jail was not going according to plan. Blade had a stronghold on the prison, and Scar's reputation on the outside didn't help him at all on the inside. He had pissed off a lot of people when he was ruling the streets, and it was now coming back to haunt him. At the rate it was going, Scar would either be someone's bitch by the end of the month, or he would be dead. He certainly wouldn't be running the joint.

"Nigga, you ain't Flex." The beatings hadn't lessened Scars attitude any.

"Nah, I ain't. Flex sent me in his place."

Scar had gotten in touch with Flex in hopes that he would be able to get some help to him on the inside.

"This some bullshit. I ain't dealin' with no corner boy. Tell that nigga I only deal with him."

"I don't think so. Flex sent me to tell you that he runnin' shit now. Your time is over. Rot in hell, mu'fucka." The boy hung up the phone and walked out of the room, leaving Scar screaming at the top of his lungs and pounding on the plexiglass until the guards restrained him.

Flex listened intently as the boy recounted the story. When he finished, Flex peeled off five hundred dollars from the knot in his pocket and handed it to the boy.

"You done good, Slam," Flex told him. "Now, let's bounce. I got a meeting. You driving." He tossed the keys to his Suburban to Slam.

The boy hid his excitement. He'd just received five hundred dollars, and now he was going to get to drive Flex around. At thirteen years old, he had never seen so much money or had so much responsibility. He and his friends had been stealing cars to go joy-riding since he was ten, so driving was nothing new to him. The excitement came from the fact that he was making something of himself, making his own money and chauffeuring the notorious Flex.

Slam pulled into the abandoned warehouse and parked the car in the center of the cavernous structure. Flex and his crew stepped out of the truck. A few minutes later, a caravan of black sedans and Suburbans with tinted windows came rolling into the warehouse. Flex and his crew stood and watched the theatrics of all the cars fanning out and coming to a synchronized stop.

After the cars had taken their places, a stretch limousine pulled in and stopped right next to Flex. Flex did nothing. He wasn't nervous, and even if he was, he wasn't about to show it. The back passenger's window rolled down.

"Get in," instructed the man in the car.

Flex took a briefcase from one of his crew and got into the limousine. Inside sat the new mayor of Baltimore. Mayor Richard Malenchek had taken over after a special election was scheduled. He won in a landslide victory, with the help of Governor Tillingham. There were rumors that the election was fixed, but there was no definitive proof.

"How are you?" the mayor asked.

"Good, good."

"Do you have something for me?" The mayor looked down at the briefcase and raised his eyebrows.

Flex passed the briefcase to Mayor Malenchek, who placed it on his lap and flipped open the latches. He ran his hand over the cash inside.

"Like we agreed?"

"Six hundred Gs," Flex answered.

"Well, good luck to you on your business venture this year. I will make sure that my administration does not interfere for the next twelve months."

"See you in a year," Flex said.

Flex and the mayor shook hands to seal their deal.

"I think this is the start of a lucrative business deal for both of us." The mayor gave a wicked smile.

Flex exited the limousine. He stood with his crew and watched the caravan drive away from the warehouse. With the mayor in his pocket for the next year, Flex was now free to take over the drug trade in Baltimore without any repercussions or backlash.

The faces may have changed, but the corruption in Baltimore would always stay the same.

Coming Soon 2012

The Block

by

Treasure Hernandez

Chapter 1

Tone sat in the passenger seat of the new Audi staring blankly out the window, stuck in his own thoughts, while his main man Maine drove. Tonight was no different from any other night. Tone had just got word on some guy named Sam that owed him some money, and he was going to make sure the man paid up. Tone was the leader of the empire that he was building from the ground up, and everybody knew he and his crew didn't play, so for Sam to be trying to duck him didn't sit well with him not one bit.

Maine pulled up in the empty parking lot and saw Sam surrounded by twelve of Tone's goons. "That's him right there?" he asked.

"Yeah, that's that nigga," Tone said in a cool tone as he stepped out the Audi, a bottle of Grey Goose in his hand. He was angry that Sam was trying to duck him, but even more so that he had to leave the comfort of his home to come out here right now. He passed the bottle of Grey Goose over to Maine as he walked up to Sam.

"Yo, fam, where's the rest of my money at?" Tone asked in a cool tone.

Sam looked at Tone and the twelve goons he had standing behind him and took a deep breath. "I got robbed," he replied, a look of shame on his face.

"Got robbed?" Tone echoed. "Fuck you mean, you got robbed? Who robbed you?"

"Gruff and that bitch Maxine," Sam answered.

Tone let out a deep breath as he turned and smacked the shit outta Sam. "Nigga, you let a nigga and a bitch rob you?"

"Nah, son, that nigga Gruff—"

"Nigga, shut the fuck up!" Tone said, quickly cutting Sam off. "Empty ya mu'fuckin' pockets right now!" he demanded.

Everybody watched Sam lower his head, take out everything he had in his pockets, and hand it to Tone.

"Yo, Maine, wash this nigga up," Tone told his best friend, whom he'd known since childhood. Immediately Maine covered his eyes as he busted the bottle of Grey Goose over Sam's head, dropping him instantly. Once the goons saw Sam's body hit the floor, they were all over him like vultures, kicking and stomping his face into the concrete.

"Mu'fucka must've thought shit was a game," Tone said out loud, stuffing the three hundred dollars that he just took from Sam into his pocket.

"How much that nigga was short?" Maine asked as him and Tone stood over on the side, and the goons continued to destroy what was left of Sam.

"Seven thousand."

Just then Tone noticed an unmarked car pull up to the scene, and seconds later out hopped a dark-skinned man with salt-and-pepper hair. From his muscular frame, you could tell that he still worked out often. Around his neck hung a shiny gold badge, and behind him was two uniformed cops.

When the goons spotted him, they immediately stopped the beating they was putting on Sam.

"Please don't stop 'cause I'm here." Detective Abraham smirked. "Fuck is going on out here?" He looked over at Tone.

"Mu'fucka owe, so he had to pay," Tone said noncha-lantly.

Detective Abraham smoothly walked over to Maine, reached inside his waistband and removed a .380 with a silencer on the muzzle. "Mu'fucka had to pay, huh?" As he stood over Sam's body, he fired three shots into his face. "What I told you about playing with mu'fuckas?" Detective Abraham growled. He slapped Tone in the back of his head. "I fuckin' taught you better than that."

"My bad, Pops," Tone said as he took the gun from his father's hand and passed it back to Maine.

"It's always your bad," Detective Abraham huffed as he walked back to his unmarked car followed by the two uniformed officers. "Be at my house first thing in the morning," he yelled over his shoulder as he slid back in his car and pulled off.

"Man, ya pops don't play," Maine said as he slid in the driver's seat of his all-black Audi.

"You know he just wants us to be the best we can be," Tone replied as he slid in the passenger seat. "He been telling me all week about this big plan he got for us. Finally, he suppose to spill the beans tomorrow."

"Well, whatever it is, you know it's a lot of paper involved," Maine said, knowing how much Detective Abraham loved money.

"Maine pulled up in front of Tone's crib and threw his car in park. "Want me to come scoop you up tomorrow?"

"Nah. Just meet me at my pop's crib at like ten." Tone gave Maine a pound and slid out the passenger seat.

As soon as Tone stepped foot in the house, he saw his high-school sweetheart Mya in front of the TV doing her daily exercise with her Nintendo Wii. As soon as she spotted Tone, she quickly paused her game and headed over toward her man. Tone smiled as he watched his sexy-ass woman strut toward him wearing nothing but green boy shorts and matching bra. Mya favored the actress Vivica Fox but had a little more ass.

"Hey, baby," she said with a smile as she slid in Tone's arms.

Tone kissed Mya on the lips and playfully pushed her off of him. "Get outta here. You all sweaty and shit."

"Shut up. You know you love my sweat." She smiled as she walked over to the TV and continued her workout.

After Tone helped himself to three shots of Grey Goose, he said, "How was your day?"

"It was okay. Had to stop these two bitches from fighting in the salon today. Other than that, it was a regular boring day," Mya told him as she jogged in place in front of the TV.

"I remember when you was begging me to get you your own salon, and now it's like you can't stand it." Tone laughed. "Women don't never know what they want."

"I love my salon. I just don't like all the people that come up there sometimes." Mya cut the TV off and headed to the bathroom so she could hop in the shower.

Tone headed over to the entertainment system and blasted Jay-Z's song, "Empire State of Mind." He sang along with Hov as he removed his .40-caliber from his waistband and sat it on the counter.

After he helped himself to another shot, he reached into his pocket and pulled out a ring box. He opened it and examined the diamond closely. He had been waiting for the perfect time to pop the question and thought tonight was the night.

"Hey," Mya said, appearing outta nowhere. "What you over there doing?" She was strolling through the house butt naked like she always did after her night shower.

"Minding my business." Tone smiled as he held the box behind his back.

Mya walked over to the entertainment system and turned the music down. "Why you always gotta have your music so damn loud?" When she turned around, her mouth hung wide open in shock.

Tone was on his knees and holding open the box with the ring. "Baby, will you marry me?"

"Yes!" Mya said loudly as she snatched the ring and put it on her finger.

Tone just smiled. He loved seeing Mya happy, but he had never seen her this happy "Well . . . do you like It?"

Mya didn't answer. Instead, she walked over to Tone, unbuckled his belt, removed his dick, and slid down to her knees.

"Awww shit!" Tone moaned as he watched his fiancée work her magic.

Mya sucked and jerked on Tone's dick until he finally released in her mouth.

"Damn, baby," he said, breathing heavily. "Thanks."

"What you thanking me for? I'm just now getting started." Mya grabbed Tone's wrist and led him into the bedroom.

The next morning Tone woke up to his cell phone ringing. "Hello," he answered in a drowsy voice.

"Get ya ass over here," his father growled into the receiver.

Tone peeked over at the digital clock on the night-stand. "It's seven o'clock. You said to be there at ten."

"Be here in twenty minutes," Detective Abraham said, ending the conversation.

"Who was that, baby?" Mya asked, her eyes still closed.

"My father." Tone sat up to start getting dressed.

"Damn!" Mya whined. "You gotta go meet him right now?"

"Yeah. But I won't be gone too long, I promise."

After brushing his teeth, Tone stuck his .40-cal in his waistband and headed out the door.

Tone walked up to his father's front door and banged on it with an attitude. He hated getting up early. His father answered the door with a smile on his face.

"What the fuck is so important that I had to get outta my warm bed so early in the morning?" Tone asked, clearly upset.

Detective Abraham kept his smile up. "The early bird always gets the worm."

"Ain't no birds up this early." Tone headed inside and sat at the kitchen table.

"You wanna make some money or not?" Detective Abraham asked as he poured himself a drink.

"What you got up your sleeve now?" Tone asked, knowing his pops was always up to something.

"This what I got up my sleeve." Detective Abraham slid a folder toward his son.

Tone opened up the folder and saw a picture of an old Spanish- looking man. "Fuck is this?"

"His name is Santiago." Detective Abraham paused before adding, "He lives in L.A. now, but he's from

Mexico. He's one of the biggest cocaine distributors in
the world."

"So what you need me to do? Kill him?"

"Impossible," Detective Abraham said quickly. "We
want to do business with him."

"So what's the big deal?" Tone asked, confused.

"The big deal is, he don't fuck with black people,"
Detective Abraham said with an angry look on his face.
He hated racists, even though he was a racist himself.

"So where do I come in at in all of this?"

"Here's where you come in at." Detective Abraham
slid his son another folder.

Tone opened the folder and saw a picture of a beautiful woman inside. "Who this?"

"That's Santiago's daughter, Serena."

"What does she have to do with anything?" Tone
didn't like whatever his father was up to.

"She's in town for two weeks on vacation. She's staying at the New Yorker Hotel on Thirty-Fourth Street."

"And?"

"And you got two weeks to get in her head and convince her that you love her. Then once you get in good
enough, you can get her to convince her father to do
business with us." Detective Abraham smiled like he
had everything all figured out.

"I don't know about this one, Pops," Tone said in
deep thought.

"What's not to know? You wanna make some big
money, right?"

"Yeah, but—"

"But nothing. It's a perfect plan."

"I ain't gon' be able to stay out the house for two
weeks. Mya would kill me. Plus, we just got engaged
last night."

"Fuck Mya! With the type of money you gonna be making, you can buy two more Myas." Detective Abraham chuckled, but he was dead serious.

But Tone didn't appreciate his father's remark about Mya. "Must you talk foolish all the time?"

"You know I was joking with you," Detective Abraham said, trying to downplay his comment. "All I'm saying is, you know Mya is a ride-or-die chick, so just explain to her what it is you gonna be doing, and you'll be fine."

"It ain't that easy, Pops. Mya is super jealous. I can't just say, 'Hey, baby, I'ma be fucking another bitch for two weeks,' and think she gonna be cool with that."

"Stop bitching and man up." Detective Abraham downed his drink in one gulp, only to refill his glass back up to the top. "You wanna make this money or what?"

"How much paper you think we can make if I can make this chick think I'm in love with her?"

"Millions!" Detective Abraham's eyes lit up just thinking about that amount of money. He didn't know how, but he had to make his son see what he saw, and he wasn't going to stop until he accomplished that mission.

"Damn! Two weeks is a short amount of time to make a bitch fall in love," Tone said out loud as he helped himself to a drink.

"I thought you was a pimp," Detective Abraham joked. "My name is John Abraham, and your name is Anthony Abraham. You know what that means?"

Tone smiled. "What?"

"That means you can do anything you put your mind to . . . trust me."

Detective Abraham heard somebody knocking at his front door. "Who is it?" he yelled, walking over to the door. He smiled when he saw Maine standing on the other side of the door. "Come on in."

"Y'all in here having a secret meeting without me?" Maine jokingly.

"Nah. Just going over a few things with this knucklehead over there." Detective Abraham motioned his head toward his son. "Speaking of knuckleheads . . . what was all that about last night?"

"That clown, Sam, owed us some bread, so we had to beat it outta him."

Maine loved putting in work and would do it for free, so getting paid for it was just a bonus.

"Nigga said some clown named Gruff robbed him, and some bitch named Maxine helped him," Tone told him.

"Who Gruff? From Brooklyn?" Detective Abraham asked, his voice rising a bit.

"Yeah, I think so," Tone answered. "Why? You know him?"

"I can't stand that muthafucka," Detective Abraham fumed. "Before I became a detective, I had many run-ins with that clown. Even whipped his ass once, me and my partner in an alley." He shook his head. "He ain't nothing but a trigger-happy nigga, in it for a street rep. He don't even care about the money."

"So what's up with him now?" Maine asked.

"Last I heard, he was on the run for some attempted murder charge," Detective Abraham said.

"What about the Maxine bitch?" Tone asked.

Detective Abraham shrugged his shoulders. "Never heard of her. She must be a new jack."

"Well, we ain't gotta worry about shit 'cause I'm gonna hunt that Gruff nigga down personally." Maine smirked.

"Let me just warn you," Detective Abraham said seriously as he placed his gaze on Maine, "that nigga Gruff gets busy."

"Good. 'Cause I get busy too," Maine said, a smirk still on his face.

"Fuck that clown Gruff," Detective Abraham said, waving him off. "I'ma need you focused 'cause you gonna be running shit for a while."

"Word?" Maine asked excitedly. "Why? What's up?"

"I put ya man Tone here on a mission that's going to last for a few weeks, so until then, you the man. Now both of y'all get the fuck outta here and make me proud," he said, dismissing the two.

Tone stepped out of his father's house not knowing how to feel. He wanted to make the money, but on the other hand, he didn't want Mya to be mad at him, or this job to ruin his healthy relationship. He knew Mya wasn't going to go for that shit, no matter how much money was involved.

"What's good? You a'ight?" Maine asked, sensing something was wrong.

"I'm good," Tone lied.

"What's good? You wanna run downtown with me? I'm supposed to be looking at this new car."

"Nah. I gotta head downtown to the New Yorker Hotel." Tone slid in his Benz and disappeared from his father's driveway.

Chapter 2

Tone pulled up in front of the New Yorker Hotel and let his engine die. "Fuck!" he said out loud as he grabbed the folder and took out the woman's picture to examine it. He tossed the picture back in the folder and leaned his head back against the headrest and waited patiently for his prey to either come in or exit the hotel.

Five hours later he saw the woman exit the hotel. "Damn!" He thought she was much prettier in person. The woman resembled the singer Keri Hilson, except for her hair that came down to the middle of her back. Her tall black boots made her calves and legs look toned and sexy. Just from looking at her, Tone could tell that she was stuck up and used to the finer things in life.

He quickly made the engine of his Benz come to life with one turn of his key when his mark hopped in a yellow cab. He pulled out of his parking spot and followed the cab. After a short drive, the cab stopped at Forty-Second Street. Tone continued to follow the woman and watched her walk into Applebee's. He quickly pulled off and found a parking garage around the corner, where he parked his car, and headed over to Applebee's.

He walked inside the restaurant and saw his mark sitting over in a booth by the window looking through the menu.

"Just one?" the waitress politely asked him.

"Yeah." Tone followed the waitress over to a booth on the other side of the restaurant. "Excuse me, but is it possible for me to sit over there with that woman?" he asked.

"Well, sir, that's up to her," the waitress said, a confused look on her face.

"A'ight." Tone walked over and slid in the opposite side of the booth his mark was sitting at.

Serena sat in the booth over in the corner looking over her menu. She was starving and ready to eat. So far she'd been enjoying her vacation in New York. Her father always made sure she had the best of everything, and this time was no different. Once she decided what she wanted to eat, she looked up for the waitress. That's when she saw a handsome man heading over in her direction. He favored the singer Trey Songz but was a little rough around the edges. Serena watched as the man slid in her booth and sat opposite her.

"Can I help you?" she asked in a snotty tone.

"Oh, what's up?" Tone asked as he picked up the menu and began looking inside.

"Umm, can I help you?" Serena said, raising an eyebrow. "I mean, this is my table."

"I'm just tryin'a get something to eat and didn't wanna eat by myself." Tone paused. "And I saw a beautiful lady over here eating alone, so I thought, why not eat together?" He shrugged his shoulders.

Serena rolled her eyes. "How you know I wasn't waiting for someone?"

"Are you waiting for somebody?"

"That ain't the point," she said with a smile.

Tone returned her smile. "Nah, but for real, I had to come over here and talk to you. I've yet to see a woman as beautiful as you in my life. You must be from out of town, 'cause ain't no chicks out here that look like you."

"Yeah, I am from out of town, but beauty is only skin deep," Serena said in her West Coast accent.

The waitress walked up to the table, interrupting the conversation. "Are y'all ready to order?"

"Yes, ma'am," Tone said politely. "Can I have a steak, some French fries, and some rice, please?" he said as he handed the waitress back the menu.

The waitress looked at Serena. "And you, ma'am?"

"Yes, can I have some chicken fingers and some fries, please?"

"And to drink?"

Before Serena could say a word, Tone quickly replied, "Two Long Island ice teas please."

"Coming right up." The waitress smiled as she turned and disappeared through the double doors.

The two ate and talked for about an hour. As they sipped on their third Long Island ice tea, Tone asked, "So how long you in town for?" though he already knew the answer.

"Two weeks."

"Damn! So I don't got much time then?"

"Much time for what?" she asked suspiciously.

"To try and convince you to stay," Tone said with a smile.

Serena chuckled. "I like New York, but that doesn't mean I wanna live here."

"I can dig it." Tone smiled. "So what you doing later on?"

"Nothing. Probably just gonna sit in my room and watch movies all night."

"Fuck that!" Tone said, canceling her movie night. "I'm taking you out tonight. I'm not gonna let you spend your two weeks here just sitting up in a room."

Serena liked the way Tone was taking control, and the way he carried himself. "What did you have in mind?"

"Just be ready around eight o'clock," Tone said with a smile as him and Serena got up and exited the restaurant.

"Yo, what you doing?" Tone asked when he saw Serena trying to flag down a cab.

"Trying to get a cab," she said innocently.

"Don't disrespect me like that." Tone smiled. "Wait right there."

Five minutes later Tone pulled up to the corner in his Benz. Once Serena got in, he quickly pulled off.

Maine double-parked his Denali in front of the projects. Now that he was in charge while Tone was on that other mission, he planned on letting it be known that he was moving up in the empire and wasn't taking no shit. He walked up to a building, where about five local guys stood in front. "What's good? How's it looking out here?" Maine asked as he gave each man dap.

"Slow motion," a skinny cat named Calvin answered.

"Yo, any of y'all seen Gruff out here lately?" Maine asked.

"I saw that cat the other day," Calvin said, searching his memory.

"Word? You know where I can catch up with him at?"

"Nah. You know Gruff moves like the wind. It's hard to catch him in one spot," Calvin reminded him. "Why? Something up?"

"Nah, we cool. I just got something I need to give him," Maine said as he headed in the building.

After waiting a few minutes for the elevator, Maine decided to take the stairs to the fifth floor. He walked down the hall until he found the door he was looking for. He knocked and waited for a reply. He heard somebody fiddling with the locks. A man with a messed-up Afro opened the door and stepped to the side for Maine to enter.

"Damn, nigga! Why it always smell like ass when I come up in here?" Maine huffed, his nose wrinkled up.

"Fuck outta here! I ain't smell shit until you got here," Afro capped back.

"Man, just gimme what you got for me, so I can get up outta here." Maine covered his mouth and nose with his shirt as he watched Afro head toward the back.

Afro returned with a book bag. "Take this and get the fuck out! Coming up in here, funking my shit all up with that cheap-ass cologne you got on." He escorted Maine to the door. Every time him and Maine got together the two would go at it.

"Fuck outta here!" Maine said, walking out the apartment. "Nigga, you smell like a dead body," he yelled over his shoulder and disappeared through the staircase door.

Maine slid back behind the wheel of his Denali when he heard his cell phone ringing. Instantly he recognized the number. "What's good?"

"Got a little problem I need you to solve for me," Detective Abraham told him.

"E-mail me the nigga résumé."

A minute later Maine checked the e-mail on his phone, and an address and profile picture came up of his target. He quickly punched the address in his navigational system and headed toward the destination.

Detective Abraham sat in an all-black van along with three of his crooked partners. For about two weeks, they had been scoping out Big Mike's dope house. Detective Abraham was tired of watching him get rich. He took a deep drag from his Newport. "Damn! This nigga spot is really clicking."

Maxwell, one of Abraham's crooked partners, said, "Yeah, he going to have to come up off this spot."

"Y'all muthafuckas ready?" Detective Abraham asked as he loaded his MAC-11.

All three of his partners nodded their heads yes.

"Let's do it."

Detective Abraham slid out the van and ran up toward the back door. He silently counted to three and watched Maxwell kick the back door open.

"Police! Nobody move!" Detective Abraham yelled as he stormed inside.

Big Mike tried to grab the AK-47 that sat next to him, but he quickly put the assault rifle back down when he realized they had the drop on him.

"Don't fucking move!" Detective Abraham said, his MAC-11 trained on the drug dealer.

"Fuck y'all pigs want?" Big Mike asked with an attitude. "Y'all want money, or y'all came to lock me up this time?"

"Depends." Detective Abraham smiled. "How much money you got up in here?"

"About fifty thousand. Why?"

"Hand that over," Detective Abraham said quickly.

"It's over there in the safe," Big Mike said.

Just then somebody knocked on Big Mike's door.

"That's just one of my customers," he said nonchalantly.

Maxwell looked over and saw the table covered with bundled-up dope. He grabbed a few bundles and walked to the door and served the fiend.

Detective Abraham smiled as he dialed his son's number.

On the fifth ring, Tone finally answered. "What up?"

"I need you to send me a few workers over here," Detective Abraham told him. "Got us a new spot."

"I got you. Just e-mail me the address," Tone said as he ended the call.

Once Detective Abraham hung up the phone, he quickly e-mailed Tone the info he needed.

"Y'all already got the money. Now what?" Big Mike said.

"Now you say good night."

Detective Abraham smiled as he raised his MAC-11 and pulled the trigger. The rest of the crew watched Big Mike's body jerk back and forth as the bullets ripped through him.

"Clean this mess up and call me and let me know when the workers get here." Detective Abraham walked up out the dope house like nothing never happened. This was just the beginning of his big plan. Plus, who was going to stop him? He was the police.

"A'ight," Tone said to his workers, "I need y'all over there as soon as possible. One."

As soon as he hung up the phone, Mya was all over him. "Where you going, looking all nice?"

"Looking all nice?" Tone echoed. "I got on regular clothes."

"I thought you was taking me out tonight," Mya whined. She had been waiting all day for Tone to come home so they could go out, like he had promised.

"I was, but I gotta do something for my pops tonight."

"But you promised me. Can't you do whatever it is you gotta do for him tomorrow?"

"Nah, it's gotta be done tonight. Sorry." Tone kissed Mya on her forehead. "But, I promise you, I won't be out too late." Then he stuck his .40-cal in his waistband and headed out the door.

Maine pulled up in front of the building his GPS led him to. He quickly pulled out his .380 and screwed on the silencer before exiting his whip. He walked in the building and took the stairs to the third floor. When he reached the apartment he was looking for, he flung his hood over his head as he knocked on the door. Once he saw somebody looking through the peephole, he quickly raised his gun up to it and pulled the trigger once. After Maine heard the body drop, he shot off the doorknob. Then he busted up in the apartment and shot the body that lay on the floor two more times before shutting the door behind him.

As Maine slowly eased his way through the apartment, he could hear soft R&B music coming from the back room. Holding his gun in a two-handed grip as he approached the back room, he quickly busted up in the room and saw a woman breast-feeding an infant.

He raised his gun and sent a bullet through her skull. The woman collapsed straight back on the bed, and the baby rolled out of her arms onto the floor, screaming at the top of its lungs.

Maine checked the rest of the apartment to make sure there was nobody else inside. Then he disappeared out the front door.

Maine pulled up in front of his crib and let the engine die as he stepped out the car. As soon as he walked in the door, he saw his girlfriend Monique halfway dressed, and two of her girlfriends sitting on the couch.

"Fuck you going?" he asked.

"Out," Monique replied. "You think I'm supposed to be stuck up in this house all muthafuckin' day while you just out doing whatever? I don't think so."

"I know that's right," one of her girlfriends cooed.

"I'm out getting money," Maine said, nodding down to the blood on his shoes. "And you out running the streets."

"I can't go out every now and then with my girls? Why I always gotta be 'running the streets'? You must be out doing dirt. That's probably why you never want me to go nowhere."

"You know what? Just get your shit and get the fuck out!"

Monique smiled, her hands on her hips. "You kicking me out?"

"Either get out, or get put out," Maine said in an even tone.

Monique saw the look in Maine's eyes and knew he wasn't bullshitting.

"Fuck you, nigga!"

Monique huffed as she grabbed a few things from out the back room. "Bitch-ass nigga! I was doing you a favor staying here. Talking 'bout get out or get put out—I wish you would put your muthafuckin' hands on me!"

"You see, if I had a white bitch, I wouldn't have to go through this kinda shit," Maine spat. He knew she hated to see a white woman with a black man.

"Nigga, fuck you and your white bitch! I wish I would catch you with a white bitch. I'll beat you and that bitch's ass!"

"Just get out!" Maine smirked. "And hurry the fuck up!"

"Get a good look 'cause you ain't gon' never see me or this ass again," Monique said as her and her friends left, leaving the front door wide open.

Maine closed the door and flopped down on the couch. After a long day, all he wanted to do was have a drink, get some head, and watch a movie until he fell asleep, but instead he had to come home to chaos and foolishness.

Chapter 3

Tone pulled up in front of the New Yorker Hotel and saw Serena standing out front looking super sexy. He tapped the horn twice and watched as Serena strutted toward the Benz and slid in the passenger seat.

She kissed Tone on the cheek. "I thought you was tryin'a stand me up."

"Damn! A nigga can't even be five minutes late." Tone smiled as he pulled out into traffic.

"So where we going?"

"To go eat," Tone answered quickly.

Thirty minutes later Tone pulled up to a nice soul food restaurant. "You like soul food?"

"I love soul food," Serena answered with her glossed-up lips. "I'm glad you brought me here."

"Why? What's up? You wanna go somewhere else?"

"Nah, I just don't like being around a lot of bougie people. I just like eating around down-to-earth people," she tried to explain.

"I feel you." Tone smiled.

Serena liked that the clientele at this soul food restaurant was mixed with white, black, and Spanish customers. That meant that the food was tasty, and appealing to everybody.

Once the two were seated, Serena popped the million-dollar question. "So what do you do for a living?"

Tone smiled. "You want me to lie or tell the truth?"

"Both," Serena said, matching his smile.

"Okay, I'm the local cable man, and I do electrician on the side."

"Okay, now the truth," Serena said, shaking her head and smiling.

Tone paused before he answered, "I control a big drug empire," looking at Serena for her reaction.

"Fuck it! We all gotta do what we gotta do," she said seriously.

Her response caught Tone off guard. "So you cool with that?"

"Yeah, my uncle and a few of his peoples used to fuck around in the drug game, and half of my family use drugs. So I'm no stranger to that type of stuff."

"You ever had a boyfriend that was into that lifestyle?"

"Not yet. Why you ask?"

"'Cause, as you can see, I'm really feeling you. Everything about you. I've yet to meet a woman who I can talk to on some regular shit, feel me?"

"I feel you, but this ain't gonna work."

"What you mean? Why not?"

"Because we live in two different cities. And you have a life, and so do I."

"What if I want you in my life?" Tone pressed.

"How are you so sure? You don't know me like that."

"I want to get to know you," Tone said, looking Serena in her eyes. "I don't care if I have to come out to L.A. once a month so we can be together. Whatever I have to do, I'ma do it."

Serena smirked. "I hear you talking."

"I let my actions do my talking," Tone countered.

The two ate their food and sat and talked for about forty-five minutes in the restaurant before leaving. As they walked back to the car, Tone felt his phone vibrating. He looked at the caller ID and saw that it was Mya. He quickly put his phone on silent as he put it back in the case.

"So what you got planned for the rest of the night?" Tone asked as he slid in the driver's seat.

"Go back to my room and get some rest."

"You want some company?"

"That would be nice." Serena smiled. "But that don't mean you getting none of this good pussy."

Tone smirked. "I just wanna spend as much time with you as I can before you leave," he said as he pulled into traffic.

As the two drove chitchatting, a crackhead flagged the Benz down like his life depended on it.

"Fuck!" Tone huffed as he quickly pulled over to the side of the road and rolled his window down.

Serena was about to say something but decided to just keep quiet.

The crackhead ran up to the driver's window all out of breath. "Tone, wassup, man? I thought that was you," he said, trying to fix the collar on his shirt.

"Fuck you doing out here, Malcolm?" Tone asked, not looking the fiend directly in his eyes.

"Just out tryin'a get some fresh air." Malcolm wiped the slime from the corners of his mouth. "You got a few dollars you can spare so I can go get me something to eat?"

Tone pulled five twenties from his knot and handed them to Malcolm. "Swing by my house tomorrow night so we can get you straightened up."

"Okay, I got you." Malcolm hurried off across the street.

Tone pulled off, a frown on his face.

"You okay?" Serena asked.

"Yeah, I'm fine," he huffed. "It just bothers me to see him all fucked up like that."

"He a close friend of yours?"

"Nah, that's my brother."

"Oh, I'm sorry to hear that."

"It's all good," Tone said as he pulled up in front of the New Yorker Hotel.

"You still coming up?" Serena asked.

"Nah, I'm about to go back and try to find my brother before he gets himself killed," Tone said, a sad look on his face.

"Okay. You know where I'm at if you need me." Serena kissed Tone on his cheek and headed inside the hotel.

As soon as she disappeared inside the hotel, Tone pulled out his cell phone and dialed his pops' number.

"What you want?" Detective Abraham grumbled into the receiver.

"I just saw Malcolm out here."

"Fuck you telling me for?"

"Maybe because that's your son."

"That muthafucka ain't my son!"

"Malcolm out here looking real bad, Pops. He needs our help."

"Fuck Malcolm! I done helped that boy as much as I can. Once a muthafucka steal out my house, he ain't considered family no more. He lucky I didn't kill his ass!"

"He's still your son, no matter what."

"The only son I got is you, and if you start getting high, then fuck you too!" Detective Abraham hung up in Tone's ear.

"Ignorant muthafucka!"

***

As soon as Tone stepped foot in the crib, he found Mya sitting in the living room waiting for him, a scarf on her head and her arms folded. "So we not answering phones now?"

"Not tonight, baby, please," Tone said as he walked in the kitchen.

Mya quickly shot to her feet. "Fuck you mean, not tonight? You gon' tell me something."

"I was out and ran into Malcolm," Tone said, pouring himself some orange juice.

Mya knew the deal about his brother's bad crack problem and felt bad about it. "How is he?" she said, her whole tone changing.

"He look bad. I just hate to see him all fucked up and shit. No matter what I do to try and help, it seems like nothing works."

"He ain't gonna get that monkey off his back until he's ready to," Mya said, rubbing her man's back. "Trust me, only he'll know when enough is enough."

"You right."

After Tone went to the back, took a shower, and got in the bed, Mya hopped on his dick and rode it like there was no tomorrow, until the two both came then fell fast asleep in each other's arms.

Chapter 4

"So, what I been missing?" Tone sipped on some vodka and orange juice. He looked around the warehouse and saw about ten to twelve soldiers just sitting around, telling lies and war stories.

"You ain't really been missing shit." Maine, who was drinking his vodka straight, downed his drink. "Your pops done busted mad drug dealers and took over their spots."

"Word?"

"Yeah. So, I put a few soldiers in each spot." Maine picked up the new machine gun he had just purchased and started tinkering with it. "But what's good with you and that honey?"

"She cool." Tone sipped his drink. "I think I can pull it off."

"Well, shit. At least you gon' get some pussy out of the deal." Maine smiled. "I heard she fine too."

Tone smiled. "Yeah, she good money."

"Yeah, I bet."

Just then Maine's cell phone started ringing. He answered, "Yeah, who this?"

"Yo, this Li'l Man. That nigga Gruff out here in the projects right now. Get down here fast 'cause I think he about to leave."

"Be there in a minute." Maine hung up the phone, grabbed his new machine gun, and headed toward the door.

"Yo," Tone called out, "where you going?"

"Just got the drop on that clown Gruff. I'll be back in a second," he said as he disappeared out the door.

Tone shook his head. He smiled when he saw Serena's name flashing across the screen of his cell phone. "What's good, ma?" he answered.

"You tell me," she capped back. "I was just calling to see what was up for tonight."

"I mean, what you wanna do? You know I'm down for whatever," Tone told her.

"I think I wanna go out tonight, so put on your dancing shoes and come pick me up tonight."

"Say no more. I got you. I'll see you in about two hours."

"A'ight, I'll be waiting."

Maine pulled up to the projects and double-parked his car on the ave and hopped out with his hoodie on, one hand tucked in his pocket. He wasn't there to play no games, and couldn't wait to teach this street punk they called Gruff a lesson he would never forget. Immediately he walked straight up to Li'l Man. "What's good? Gruff still out here?"

"You just missed him," Li'l Man said with a smirk on his face.

"Something funny?"

"Nah, I'm just saying . . . what you looking for Gruff for? That nigga looked like he just killed ten people."

Maine gave Li'l Man a comical look. He thought he sounded like a bitch. "So what? You his cheerleader now?"

"Nah, I'm just saying, I did time with him back in the day, and he a cool-ass nigga."

"Let me ask you a question"—Maine stepped in Li'l Man's face—"Gruff putting money in ya fuckin' pocket?"

"Nah, it's not even—"

Maine quickly stole on the li'l nigga, knocking him out with one punch. "Bum-ass nigga," he mumbled as he stepped over Li'l Man's body and hopped back in his whip. "I'm tired of playing with these niggas," he said to nobody in particular as he headed over to the crib of one of Tone's workers to go pick up some paper that he owed.

"You not leaving out this house another night until you tell me what's going on," Mya said, standing in front of the door so Tone couldn't leave.

"What is you talking about?" Tone huffed. He knew sooner or later this moment was going to come. "Move out the way."

"Fuck you!" Mya spat, not budging. "You done been out to the wee hours in the morning for the past three days, you gon' tell me something."

"Okay, okay. I been kicking it with this chick for the last three days."

Mya smirked as she threw her hair in a raggedy ponytail. "You been doing what?" She charged him, swinging.

Tone grabbed Mya's arms and wrestled her down to the floor and sat on top of her. "Chill."

"All the shit we done been through, and you out with another bitch?" Mya growled, struggling to get up off the floor.

"Listen!" Tone yelled in her face. "I have to spend time with her. Her father is a big-time cat, and we just need her to feel comfortable with me so she can plug me in, that's all."

"Who the fuck is 'we'?"

"My pops."

"He always getting you in some shit. Why the fuck can't you ever tell him no?" Mya asked, tears escaping from her eyes. She hated Tone's father, who was always influencing him to do some dumb shit. If it wasn't one, it was another.

"Baby, this shit is only gonna take two weeks, I promise you."

"What about us?"

"What you mean?" Tone asked, confused.

"We just got engaged the other day. How you just gonna be fuckin' with another woman? Did you even take the time out to think about how I would feel?" Mya didn't wait for him to reply before she added, "If I was out for two weeks with another man, how the fuck would you feel?"

"Listen, I gotta do what I gotta do, point-blank. This is too much money to pass up on."

"Oh, so now you a prostitute? 'Cause a prostitute will do anything for money, so I guess you a prostitute."

Tone sighed loudly as he got up off Mya and headed for the door.

"You walk out that door, you ain't gotta worry about coming back," Mya said, hoping to stop her fiancé from leaving, but Tone just walked straight out the door.

"Fuck you!" she spat as she tossed the ring he had just given her a few nights before at the back of his head. "Take that piece a shit with you, you punk-ass bitch!" she yelled and slammed the door.

Tone hopped in his all-black Range Rover and pulled out the driveway. He couldn't believe how Mya was acting. As much as they had been through, he couldn't understand why she couldn't just hold it down for two weeks. She knew she was the one he wanted to marry, so what was the big deal?

Bitches always care more about love than money. But if a nigga didn't have shit and still lived with his mother, then we wouldn't've even had a relationship to start with. Fuck that! Ain't no bitch 'bout to fuck up my money. He popped in 50 Cent's new CD. *Once I get all this money, sho'll love me again in two weeks,* he thought to himself as he hit the highway, headed downtown to pick Serena up.

Maine stood in the lobby waiting for the elevator. "This shit need to hurry up," he said. In a rush to get to the strip club, he was ready to just chill for the rest of the night, get drunk, and see some freaks. He stepped on the elevator and pressed the floor he was headed to repeatedly. Once the elevator reached his floor, he stepped off and found himself looking down the barrels of two 9 mm's.

"I heard you was looking for me," Gruff said with a smile. "I would've ran down on you sooner, but I didn't even know what you looked like until earlier."

Meanwhile, Gruff's partner in crime, Maxine, stripped Maine of his .380 with the silencer on it.

Maine peeped that both stickup kids wore all black. Gruff wore a hoodie that right there told him that he didn't play, because he didn't even bother to hide his face.

"Nigga, get ya bitch ass over here!" Maxine growled. She grabbed Maine by the collar of his shirt and pushed him in front of the door he was looking for. "Knock, muthafucka!"

Maine wanted to turn around and knock the little bitch with the tough-guy talk the fuck out, but he knew at that moment he couldn't. So he did as he was told and knocked on the door.

Immediately, Rodney opened the door. "Damn, nigga! What the fuck took you so damn long?"

Gruff quickly tossed one of his 9s in Rodney's face. "Back up, playboy!" he said, busting his way up in the apartment and shoving Rodney to the floor. He quickly duct-taped Rodney's hands.

Gruff then turned his attention on Maine. "Fuck you out here looking for me for?"

"You took something that belonged to me from someone else," Maine answered.

"That sound like ya man's problem." Gruff smiled. "Fuck that gotta do with me and you?"

"I'm the enforcer," Maine answered simply.

"So you just doing your job, right?"

"Yeah"

"Me too." Gruff nodded at Maxine, who hit Maine upside his head with her .357.

Maine turned and tried to charge the bitch, but Gruff quickly put a bullet in his leg, dropping him instantly.

"Yo, fam, where you keep that money at?" Gruff asked, looking at Rodney.

"In the kitchen under the sink," he answered quickly, not wanting to get shot like Maine.

Maxine quickly walked over to the kitchen and retrieved the money.

"Listen, Maine," Gruff said, squatting so Maine could hear him clearly, "don't take this personal, but I'm just doing my job. Either respect it or check it!" Then him and Maxine headed for the door.

Before Maxine exited the apartment, she walked over and kicked Maine in his face.

Maine lay on the floor holding his bloody leg. He was mad that he had got caught slipping, but he smiled because he was still alive. He knew that the two stickup kids would definitely see him again. He struggled to his feet and leaned up against the wall for support and eased his way up out of the apartment.

"Yo, untie me," Rodney yelled at Maine's departing back, but Maine ignored him.

Detective Abraham sat on his couch watching a young sexy stripper entertain him. He hated strip clubs, 'cause there was always too many people around. He liked his shows private and in his house. That way, once the show was over, he could fuck the stripper right in his house instead of in some champagne room.

The young sexy stripper bent over and jiggled her titties in Abraham's face while he palmed her ass and whispered pervert shit in her ear. His whisper came to an end when he heard somebody banging on the door like the police.

"What the fuck?" Detective Abraham pushed the stripper out of his face and removed a .44 Magnum from under the couch cushion. He eased his way to the door. "Who the fuck is it?"

"Maine!"

"Fuck you want?" Detective Abraham quickly snatched open the door.

"Yo, I need your help," Maine said, helping himself inside, blood dripping everywhere.

Immediately Detective Abraham helped Maine to the kitchen and, with one swipe, knocked everything off the countertop and helped Maine get up there.

He looked over and saw the stripper fully dressed. "Fuck!" he said under his breath. He walked over to her and handed her a hundred-dollar bill. "Baby, I gotta take care of a li'l something, as you can see, but make sure you call me tomorrow."

The stripper kissed Detective Abraham on the cheek and promised she'd call him the next day then made her exit.

Detective Abraham quickly picked up his house phone and called a crooked street doctor that had been in the family for years. After he hung up the phone, he said to Maine. "What the fuck happened to you?"

Maine looked over Detective Abraham and, through clenched teeth, said, "Gruff!"

The club was jumping when Tone and Serena stepped foot inside. Serena danced a little bit, while Tone just stood by the wall drinking some Alizé straight from the bottle, just enjoying the scene. Dancing was never really his thing.

Serena smiled. "Come and dance with me."

"Nah, chill. That's not even my flow." Tone threw his bottle up again.

"Pleasssssse?" Serena sang as she grabbed his hand and pulled him out to the dance floor.

As Tone headed toward the dance floor, he could feel the eyes of all the other hustlers on Serena. When they got to the dance floor, Serena placed her soft ass on his dick and began grinding and gyrating her hips to the beat like she was having sex. Tone grabbed Serena's waist with one hand and started grinding even harder into her as he turned up his bottle again. The two danced for four songs straight before Tone headed back over by the wall, where he continued to watch Serena enjoy herself.

Tone felt his cell phone vibrating on his hip. He removed it from its case and read the text message that his pops had sent him:

Somebody crossed Maine up and hit him with a jump shot get here asap

Just as Tone was putting his phone back in its case, Serena walked up. "You enjoying yourself?" She took the Alizé bottle from Tone and took a deep swig.

"Something just came up, and we gotta go." Tone grabbed Serena's hand and led her out of the club.

Once outside, Serena asked, "You sure everything is okay?"

"My homie just got shot."

Just then Tone saw some big, dirty nigga named Big Phil. Tone always saw Big Phil around, but the two never spoke to each other. Big Phil was a nigga who talked big shit and liked to put on a show for the crowd. He was also known as being a disrespectful motherfucker. Immediately Tone saw Big Phil's eyes land on Serena.

Big Phil stopped dead in his tracks and shook his head. "Now that's what you call a ass," he said, craning his neck to get a better look at Serena's ass.

Tone stepped toward Big Phil. "Fuck you just say?" Tone wasn't mad about what Big Phil said, he was mad 'cause he felt that Big Phil was trying to disrespect him in front of a crowd.

"Fuck is you getting all hot for? I was just giving your joint a compliment," Big Phil said. "But if you wanna get ignorant, that ain't no problem either." He lifted his shirt and exposed the butt of his gun.

Immediately Serena jumped in front of Tone. "Let's go, baby. He ain't worth it. I'm not gonna let you go to jail over this loser," she said as she escorted him through the parking lot.

"Yeah, that's what I thought," Big Phil said loud enough so Tone and Serena could hear him. "You better listen to your bitch and get outta here before you get hurt."

Tone reached his whip and quickly grabbed his .40-cal from underneath the seat.

Before he could turn around, Serena was right in front of him. "Let it go, please," she pleaded. "It's not worth it."

Tone sighed loudly as he slid behind the wheel. Once Serena hopped in the passenger seat, he quickly pulled off. If Serena wasn't with him, he would've gone back and blown Big Phil's head off for trying to play him like that, but for the moment he had to suck it up and let it go. He knew he would definitely run into Big Phil again, and it would be more than words being exchanged.

Notes

Notes

ORDER FORM
URBAN BOOKS, LLC
78 E. Industry Ct
Deer Park, NY 11729

Name:(please print):_____

Address: _____

City/State: _____

Zip: _____

QTY	TITLES	PRICE

Shipping and handling-add $3.50 for 1st book, then $1.75 for each additional book.
Please send a check payable to:
Urban Books, LLC
Please allow 4-6 weeks for delivery

ORDER FORM
URBAN BOOKS, LLC
78 E. Industry Ct
Deer Park, NY 11729

Name: (please print): _____

Address: _____

City/State: _____

Zip: _____

QTY	TITLES	PRICE
	16 On The Block	$14.95
	A Girl From Flint	$14.95
	A Pimp's Life	$14.95
	Baltimore Chronicles	$14.95
	Baltimore Chronicles 2	$14.95
	Betrayal	$14.95
	Black Diamond	$14.95
	Black Diamond 2	$14.95
	Black Friday	$14.95
	Both Sides Of The Fence	$14.95
	Both Sides Of The Fence 2	$14.95
	California Connection	$14.95

Shipping and handling-add $3.50 for 1st book, then $1.75 for each additional book.
Please send a check payable to:
Urban Books, LLC
Please allow 4-6 weeks for delivery

ORDER FORM
URBAN BOOKS, LLC
78 E. Industry Ct
Deer Park, NY 11729

Name: (please print):_____

Address: _____

City/State: _____

Zip: _____

QTY	TITLES	PRICE
	California Connection 2	$14.95
	Cheesecake And Teardrops	$14.95
	Congratulations	$14.95
	Crazy In Love	$14.95
	Cyber Case	$14.95
	Denim Diaries	$14.95
	Diary Of A Mad First Lady	$14.95
	Diary Of A Stalker	$14.95
	Diary Of A Street Diva	$14.95
	Diary Of A Young Girl	$14.95
	Dirty Money	$14.95
	Dirty To The Grave	$14.95

Shipping and handling-add $3.50 for 1st book, then $1.75 for each additional book.

Please send a check payable to:

Urban Books, LLC

Please allow 4-6 weeks for delivery

ORDER FORM
URBAN BOOKS, LLC
78 E. Industry Ct
Deer Park, NY 11729

Name: (please print): _____

Address: _____

City/State: _____

Zip: _____

QTY	TITLES	PRICE
	Gunz And Roses	$14.95
	Happily Ever Now	$14.95
	Hell Has No Fury	$14.95
	Hush	$14.95
	If It Isn't love	$14.95
	Kiss Kiss Bang Bang	$14.95
	Last Breath	$14.95
	Little Black Girl Lost	$14.95
	Little Black Girl Lost 2	$14.95
	Little Black Girl Lost 3	$14.95
	Little Black Girl Lost 4	$14.95
	Little Black Girl Lost 5	$14.95

Shipping and handling-add $3.50 for 1st book, then $1.75 for each additional book.
Please send a check payable to:
Urban Books, LLC
Please allow 4-6 weeks for delivery

ORDER FORM
URBAN BOOKS, LLC
78 E. Industry Ct
Deer Park, NY 11729

Name: (please print):_____

Address: _____

City/State: _____

Zip: _____

QTY	TITLES	PRICE
	Loving Dasia	$14.95
	Material Girl	$14.95
	Moth To A Flame	$14.95
	Mr. High Maintenance	$14.95
	My Little Secret	$14.95
	Naughty	$14.95
	Naughty 2	$14.95
	Naughty 3	$14.95
	Queen Bee	$14.95
	Say It Ain't So	$14.95
	Snapped	$14.95
	Snow White	$14.95

Shipping and handling-add $3.50 for 1st book, then $1.75 for each additional book.
Please send a check payable to:
    Urban Books, LLC
Please allow 4-6 weeks for delivery

ORDER FORM
URBAN BOOKS, LLC
78 E. Industry Ct
Deer Park, NY 11729

Name:(please print):_____

Address: _____

City/State: _____

Zip: _____

QTY	TITLES	PRICE
	Spoil Rotten	$14.95
	Supreme Clientele	$14.95
	The Cartel	$14.95
	The Cartel 2	$14.95
	The Cartel 3	$14.95
	The Dopefiend	$14.95
	The Dopeman Wife	$14.95
	The Prada Plan	$14.95
	The Prada Plan 2	$14.95
	Where There Is Smoke	$14.95
	Where There Is Smoke 2	$14.95

Shipping and handling-add $3.50 for 1st book, then $1.75 for each additional book.
Please send a check payable to:
Urban Books, LLC
Please allow 4-6 weeks for delivery